P9-DFN-639

Also by Simon Rich

Ant Farm

Free-Range Chickens

Elliot Allagash

Miracle Workers

Man Seeking Woman

Spoiled Brats

Hits and Misses

NEW TEETH

NEW TEETH

Stories

SIMON RICH

Little, Brown and Company

New York Boston London

Little, Brown and Company
Hachette Book Group
1290 Avenue of the Americas, New York, NY 10104
littlebrown.com

First Edition: July 2021

These stories were previously published in slightly different form: "Learning the Ropes" at newyorker.com and "Raised by Wolves" and "Everyday Parenting Tips" in *The New Yorker.* "Screwball" was an Audible Original.

The photograph of the 1914 Baltimore Orioles AA International League Spring Training appeared in *Spalding's Base Ball Guide* (March 1915), published by American Sports Publishing Co.; the photograph of the 1921 Baltimore Orioles was taken by Edgar G. Moorehead, August 22, 1921.

ISBN 978-0-316-53668-4
LCCN 2020951175

LSC-C

Printing 1, 2021

Printed in the United States of America

For my wife and daughters

CONTENTS

LEARNING THE ROPES

I am me own master and commander. I serve no king and fear no God. I would sooner cut a hundred throats than heed one order from a living man. When I strike, I take no quarter, for there be no mercy in me heart, just cold, black ice. Me cutlass is me only friend. The devil is me brother. I don't recycle. When I'm done with a bottle, I just be throwing it out. I am Black Bones the Wicked, the most evil, fearsome pirate ever known.

The only man I trust is me first mate, Rotten Pete the Scoundrel, and I only trust him as far as I can keep me eye peeled on his hook hand. Rotten Pete is so rotten, he'd sell his mother for a piece of eight. He's got a black beard right up to his eyes, and he loves to keep it slick with dead men's blood. One thing about him is that he be lactose intolerant, so there be certain things he can't be eating. But other than that, he has no weaknesses, and like me, in his heart there be no mercy, just the cold, black ice, like I be having.

For years, we be charting a bloody course across the briny blue, looting every schooner fool enough to drift into our ken. When we capture a prize, we spend all the plunder on grog and sing shanties until dawn. Then we go somewhere that be open early serving breakfast. And everyone gives us dirty looks, because our table be loud, but we do not care, because we be pirates, and what makes pirates pirates is we only ever think about ourselves.

Our tale begins on the *Delicious,* a three-masted frigate built for shipping sugar biscuits. We'd hornswoggled the captain into crewing us by claiming we was common merchant seamen. But as soon as we sailed past the breakers, we whipped out our pistols and announced our true intentions.

"Ahoy!" we said. "We be pirates!"

At this point, the crew got angry at the captain for crewing us, and he got defensive-like and said, "How was I supposed to know these gentlemen were pirates?" And his crew pointed out some "red flags" me and Rotten Pete be having, like our peg legs, and our eye patches, and the parrot I be keeping on me shoulder, which always be saying, "Shiver me timbers," which be a pretty pirate thing to say. And the captain's face turned red-like and he admitted that he probably should have been getting him some references.

So, anyway, we made him walk the plank, along with all his hoity-toity educated officers. And that's when I took out me treasure map. I'd won it in a dice game against Blackjack the Crazy, and it gave us directions to all the buried gold in the known world. I nailed it to the mainmast, and we gathered around and stared at it in the boiling midday sun. And after some time, I cleared me throat and said, "So, does anyone here be knowing how to read?" And there were some groans and cursing, and I realized maybe it had been a mistake to be killing all the educated officers.

In any case, with our treasure quest at a momentary standstill, there was nothing to do but get three sheets to the wind. So Rotten Pete broke into the captain's berth by smashing the door down with his face, and we drank up all the grog and sang ourselves some shanties, with me singing the main parts, and Rotten Pete doing all the harmonies, and we were trying to work out a difficult bridge section when we heard a strange howling noise coming from the deck. It could only mean one thing: we had ourselves a stowaway.

Now, me and Rotten Pete don't take too kindly to freeloaders. So as soon as we heard his yapping, we loaded up our pistols with the hardest bullets we could find and went up to blow the man down. The wailing was coming from a broken crate of sugar biscuits, and we were gearing up to blast the thing to bits, when some clouds parted aloft, and in the white-bright moonlight we could see two little eyes peering up at us, and that's when we noticed the stowaway be a little girl.

She was smaller than a seaman's duffel, with a tiny freckled face and a scraggly mess of hair, as wild as a clump of kelp. She wore the rags of a street urchin, and her body was smeared with crumbs and bits of sugar. She'd wandered on board from the docks, we guessed, to get at all the biscuits, and now here she was, stuck with us pirates at sea.

Now, I expected her to cower at the sight of us, because she be so small, and we be so big, and also, we be pirates. But instead, when she saw us, her lips stopped their quivering, and she sniffled a few times and blinked away her tears. And then, very slow-like, she held up her arms, squeezed her chubby fists, and looked me in me eye, and said, "Up?"

And Rotten Pete turned to me slowly and said, "Arr, I think she be asking you to pick her up." And I shook me head and snorted and said, "Arr, that be ridiculous." And Rotten Pete said, "Arr, why does it be ridiculous?" And I reminded him that I don't heed orders from any living man. I would sooner cut a hundred throats. That be like one of me main things. And Rotten Pete said, "Arr, but it's not a man, it be a little girl." And I said, if *he* wanted to pick her up, that be his business. And he said, "Arr, then I guess I will be the one of us picking her up, even though I be having a hook hand, and it be harder for me to be lifting things." And I knew he be trying to be passive-aggressive, but I did not say anything, because when he be doing that, I just be ignoring it.

And so Rotten Pete picked up the small girl, and we took her to our berth, and we wrapped her in a blanket and dried off her face, and we stared at her for a while, not really sure what to do. Because we'd been through squalls and mutinies together, been shipwrecked, shot, marooned, and left for dead. But having a kid be different. It's like, there be no manual for this.

And then the small girl started talking, and she said that she be three years old, and that she be hungry for more biscuits. And Rotten Pete pulled me aside and said, "Arr, what do you think, should we be giving her more biscuits? She has already been eating a lot of biscuits today. Maybe we only give her half a biscuit and also be making her say please first?" And I said, "What the hell is going on? We be pirates. We should just throw her overboard and feed her to the sharks." And Rotten Pete winced and said, "Arr, come on, we can't be doing that." And I asked him if he be getting soft. And he said, "Arr, no, I just be thinking, you know, if we toss her overboard at night, the sharks will come, and they might crack the hull open with their fins." So I groaned and said, "Fine, she can stay aboard tonight, but there's no way she be sleeping in our berth." And he said, "Arr, then where will we be putting her?" And I said, "Arr, we can just stick her in the hold." And he said, "Arr, it be dark down there, she will be scared and scream." And I said, "Arr, if she be screaming, we'll hear her and go down." And he said, "Arr, so will *you* go down when that happens? Or are you expecting *me* to go down?" And in the end we decided we be taking turns going down.

And it was a night like no other I have lived through, louder and more vicious than the blimeyist sou'wester. The small girl kept crying, and asking us for biscuits, and when we finally gave in and brought her some, she started asking both of us for dolls. And I kept telling her, "Arr, we be pirates, we don't be having dolls," but she would keep screaming. And so eventually, to shut her up, I gave her me peg-leg and said, "Here, this be a doll," and that worked for a spell, but then the crying started again, and Rotten Pete went down, and when he came back up, he started building something out of canvas, and I asked him what he be doing, and he said, very quietly, "Arr, I be building a doll bed for her peg-leg doll, because it be needing a bed, like how she be having a bed. It be part of the game that she be playing with her doll. And also, just so you know, the name of her peg-leg doll be Peggy, so if she be asking for Peggy, that be what she means." And by dawn, I had made up me mind that sharks or no sharks, it was time for the girl to walk the plank.

So I waited until Rotten Pete was snoring-like and I climbed over him and down into the hold. And when the little girl saw me, she held up her hands and said, "Up?" And I gave her a crooked grin and said, real ominous-like, "Arr, I be lifting you up all right." And she smiled, because she be too young for understanding subtext.

And I grabbed me peg-leg from her and screwed it back on. And she laughed and said, "Peggy spin like ballerina," and when I ignored her, she said it again, and again, and again, and again, until eventually I said, "Arr, yes, she be doing pirouettes," because it just be easier to go along with her. And as she wrapped her little arms around me neck, I noticed that her hair had a smell like biscuits, and I wondered how much of that was the biscuits she be eating and how much of it just be the way she be smelling natural-like, like how some kids just be smelling sweet, like cookies. And I realized that's probably why some parents be calling their kids "cookie," because they be small and sweet, just like a cookie. In any case, it was time to commit murder.

So I started walking aft, to toss her off the poop deck. And I was almost past the mainmast, when she pointed and said, "I see X!" And I stopped in me tracks and said, "Arr, what did you say?" And she pointed again and said, "X! I see X!" And I followed her tiny finger with me eye, and that's when I saw what she be pointing at.

The treasure map.

And by this time, Rotten Pete had climbed onto the deck, and when he saw me with the girl, he squinted and said, "Arr, what you be doing?"

And I grinned and said, "Arr, just spending some quality time with me favorite little girl in the whole world!"

So it turned out that the girl knew letters, and not only that, she knew all the sounds that they be making, like "P" be for "princess," and "S" be for "sparkles," and "L" be for "lollipop." And using this inside information, we were able to sound out some words on the map, and start to make it tell its golden tales.

Sometimes it be slow going. The girl would tell a couple of letters—"this is 'T,' this is 'R'"—but then a seagull would land on some rigging and she'd run off, chasing it. And if there be a bunch of seagulls, then she'd be getting excited, and soon she'd be pretending like she be a seagull, saying "quack, quack," and flapping her arms like wings, and sometimes it be hard to redirect her.

But then I figured out the trick of bribing her with biscuits, and pretty soon I had her doing letters all day long. And after a week or two, I figured out the first spot where I thought there be some treasure, a tiny island off the coast of Malta, or as she be calling it, "mermaid, apple, lemonade, tiara, apple."

So I set our course and had me men bear down, and before long the lookout was shouting, "Land ahoy!" We rowed our swift longboat ashore, and sure enough, the treasure was just where the map had said it was, right under the "X" for "xylophone."

And so we dug up the shiny golden coins, and bit them with our teeth like we be doing, and made fast to port, where we traded them all for grog. And Rotten Pete said, "Arr, maybe we should be trading for some other stuff, too, while we're here, like baby carrots and yogurts and things that are healthy-like for the small girl." And I said, "Arr, she has biscuits," and he said, "Arr, she can't be eating only biscuits, she will be getting cavities and scurvy." And I said, "She can eat whatever she wants because she be a pirate." And that is when I told him me big plan, which was that I was going to be raising the girl in a cool way so that she be ending up cool. And instead of making her follow rules like a landlubber, I was going to teach her to reject conformity and rebel against society and also to listen to cool bands. And Rotten Pete said, "Arr, I think maybe this new philosophy of yours be something we should be discussing together in private." And I said we could be doing that some other time, because right now it be time for a pirate feast, and I opened a fresh crate of biscuits. And Rotten Pete sighed, real dramatic-like, and walked back belowdecks. And I fed the girl the biscuits and taught her some jigs, and we stayed up all night, laughing and dancing with no cares or worries in the world.

And so we kept on sailing, from island to island, scooping up treasure and crossing all the "X"s off our list. And by the end of the month, we'd plundered so much loot that the hold almost busted from the weight of all the gold, and the carpenter had to patch the cracks with caulk. And meanwhile, the girl, she be becoming increasingly pirate-like. Like, for example, she started saying "Arr" a lot, which, I'm not sure if you're aware, is a word we pirates like often to be saying. And one sunny afternoon, in between treasure stops, I taught her how to whistle with two fingers, in the pirate way, and she got so good at it, I could hear her clean across the ship, and it got to be a kind of joke between us, like I would whistle, and then she would whistle, and we would whistle back and forth, and it became like an inside thing that we be doing. And I gave her some pirate things to wear, like a red scarf for her head, which was actually only a napkin, and a cutlass for her waistband, which was actually only a small dagger. And when Rotten Pete saw her with the dagger, he said, "Arr, she'll put an eye out." And I told him to relax, because that just be an expression, and he said, "Arr, it is not just an expression. We *both* have put eyes out. It be a very common maritime accident, and it has happened to both of us and fully changed our lives." And the girl got scared-like and started to hand Rotten Pete her dagger, but then I stuck two fingers in me mouth and whistled. And the girl whistled back and refastened the dagger to her waistband.

And later that night, I was singing shanties in the berth, and I noticed that Rotten Pete was not doing the harmonies like how he normally be doing. Like technically he be doing them, but he really be phoning them in. And I thought about letting it go, because I knew if I be saying something, it would be leading to a fight, and I was just not in the mood. But then he started hitting all these obviously flat notes, especially during the "yo ho ho"s, and eventually I just looked him in the eye and said, "Is there something you be wanting to say to me?" And he said, "Arr, no." Because he always be making me drag things out of him. But after some prodding, he threw up his hook hand and said, "Arr, I am just tired of always having to be the bad guy with her." And I told him that it was not me fault that he be so neurotic-like. And he said, "Arr, it is not neurotic to try to give her a few rules." And I reminded him that we be pirates, and pirates hate rules. And he said, "Arr, I be aware, but she's not a pirate, she be a small girl who needs structure and routine to feel safe, and she be on this ship for months, and we do not even have her on any kind of sleep schedule." And then he started listing all of the things that I be doing wrong, like how me biscuits be giving her tummy aches, and me cursing be setting a bad example, and me stories about me graphic murders be making her traumatized-like, and I said, "Arr, or maybe you just be getting jealous, because she be liking me more." And the moment I said it, I knew that I be pushing things too far, but it be too late to take it back, so I just be doubling down, and from that point on, the fight just grew and grew, getting darker and murkier, like the waves in a mighty squall. And it got so bad we decided to bunk in different berths that night. And of course I know the old saying, about how a captain and first mate should never be going to bed angry, but I just be thinking to meself, "Arr, we are never going to resolve this tonight, we are both extremely tired, let's just try again tomorrow when we both be more clearheaded-like."

So I crawled out of the berth and climbed down to the lower deck, and that is when I see the water. It be seeping on up through the hold, dripping and drabbing through the waxy sealing. And when I open the latch to take a look, it be rushing out so quick, it almost knocks me peg leg loose. And when I peer down into the hold, I see the whole thing be flooded, and the small girl be sitting atop a keg of grog, just bobbing around, confused-like.

So Rotten Pete ran down and grabbed her while I sounded the alarm, ordering all hands on deck. And we manned the pumps and bailers until dawn, with the ship listing almost to beam ends. And it got so bad, the only way to keep us from a death roll was to counterflood the hold, and by the time we got the ship to sail straight, we be losing all our hard-won treasure, every single bit of gold sinking down to Davy Jones's locker. And it was the most painful moment of me pirate career, not counting that one time an octopus bit off me leg.

So I started cursing at the carpenter, because he said he'd caulked the cracks, but we ended up having more holes than a dragnet! And he swore that he'd sealed all the leaks, and said that there must be some "new holes." So I said, "Arr, well, there's going to be one *more* new hole, and it's going to be the one I be making in your chest when I be stabbing you there, right now, real hard-like!" And as I said it, I knew it was not me greatest "kill line," but I did not care, because I be so angry. And I took out me cutlass and was gearing up to cleave him to the brisket, when I caught sight of the small girl's dagger, the one that I had given her, and noticed the tip was smeared yellow.

So I bent down so I could look her in the eyes, and I said, "Arr, I am only going to be asking you this once. Were you making holes in the caulk?" And the small girl started crying, and she shook her head, and I said, "Arr, now you be lying about it, too? That be even worse!" And that's when I felt a hook on me shoulder, and I turn around, and there be Rotten Pete. And he says to me, "Arr, just calm down, it's not her fault." And I said, "Arr, what are you talking about? She just lost all our treasure!" And Rotten Pete said, "Arr, I have heard about this, it be called 'limit testing.' She be acting out because she be craving discipline, and this be what happens when the environment be too permissive-like." And I said, "Arr, so you be blaming me?!" And Rotten Pete whispered, "Arr, maybe we should discuss this somewhere else, and not in front of the small girl," and he smiled at the girl and said, "Arr, me and Black

Bones just be having a discussion, and this be a healthy thing grown-ups be doing, and everything be okay," and the little girl sniffled and nodded. And I rolled me eye and said, "Arr, I guess you be perfect, and I be horrible, congratulations." And Rotten Pete said, "Arr, I am not saying you be horrible, I am just saying that this proves that she be wanting rules." And I said, "That be ridiculous, she hates rules!" And Rotten Pete said, "Arr, or maybe you just hate giving them to her?" And the whole crew went "Ooh," which kind of spurred Rotten Pete to keep on going, and he pointed his hook at me and said, "The reason you never be disciplining her is that you be afraid that she won't love you. You are worried that she will be rejecting you, like how you felt rejected as a child, and this is why you need to be in therapy, because this all be going back to your parents' divorce, which you *never* be dealing with." And I said, "Arr, I don't need to be dealing with anything! I'm a pirate!" And he said, "Arr, or maybe you're a pirate so that you don't need to be dealing with anything." And the crew said "Ooh" again, even louder this time, and I said, "Arr, I be done with this bullshit."

And I told Rotten Pete that if he think I be such a bad captain, maybe I should just abandon ship. And I grabbed me duffel and threw it in the longboat. And Rotten Pete said, "Arr, don't do this, you'll regret it."

And I told him I would be fine, because I was taking the only thing on the ship that meant anything to me, on any emotional level. And the girl smiled at me, and I said, "Arr, not you, the treasure map." And I ripped it off the mainmast. And I reminded Rotten Pete that there still be one "X" left, and it be the greatest "X" of all—the site of the legendary Dead Man's Chest. There be more gold in that chest than in all the other chests we'd found combined, and this time, I wouldn't have to be sharing it with the likes of him! And I laughed in his face as I lowered the longboat down into the sea, because I knew his waterlogged ship could never keep pace with me. The rest of the treasure would be mine, and there'd be enough to keep me in grog for a lifetime.

And Rotten Pete said, "Arr, don't you see how you just be repeating the cycle? You be leaving us, just like how your father be leaving you." And I said, "Arr, thanks for the psychobabble," real sarcastic-like, and I picked up me parrot and was headed for the longboat when the small girl held her hands out and said, "Up?" And I told her I wouldn't be picking her up anymore, because I was leaving forever and she was staying put. And when I turned me back on her, she started to whistle like I'd taught her, but I did not whistle back, I just lowered me longboat down into the sea, and as I cut the rope, I heard her shouting down letters to impress me, saying, "I know 'A'!

I know 'B'! I know 'C'!" hoping she could make me stay, but instead I started rowing, because I be a pirate, with nothing in me heart but cold black ice, and what makes pirates pirates is we only ever think about ourselves.

The Dead Man's Chest was just like I'd imagined in me dreams: large and cube-shaped. By the time I finished loading all the loot onto me longboat, the hull nearly cracked under its weight. There were doubloons and pieces of eight and even some grog, which I drank straightaway. And then I figured it be time for celebrating, so I sang me favorite shanty. But for some reason it be sounding weird to me. So I sang it higher, and then lower, and then faster, and then slower, and finally I realized the thing it be missing was the harmonies, especially during the "yo ho ho"s. And I got this pain in me chest, like how it feels when you get capsized in a squall and you're trying to swim to the surface, but you don't know which way's up. But then I drank the rest of the grog, and the shanty started sounding better. And so I grabbed me oars and set me course west, for Madagascar, because it be having a favorable gold-to-grog exchange rate. And it was around this time that I heard a small voice say, "Up." And me heart swelled like when you catch a trade wind in full sail, and I rummaged around the boat, looking for where the little girl had stowed herself away! But eventually I realized it just be me parrot talking. And it stared at me with its dull black eyes, saying, "Up! Up! Up! Up!" And so I said, "Shiver me timbers," you know, trying to get it to talk more pirate-like. But the bird kept saying, "Up!" and "I know 'A'!" and "I know 'B'!" And maybe it was the grog, or the heat, or me scurvy, or me late-stage syphilis, but I started to talk back to the parrot, just like it was a person, begging it to stop, pleading with the bird to leave me be. But instead it just got louder, asking for biscuits, and blankets for Peggy, and by the time it started whistling, I'd turned me boat around and started rowing east back to the ship. But I was moving too slow to catch up with them, on account of all me treasure, so I hurled the heavy pieces overboard, and then the medium pieces, and then some of the little pieces, too, and by the time I had the mainmast in me sights, I had only a couple pieces left. So I tossed those as well, along with me peg leg, and me cutlass, and me earrings, scarf, and pistols, and me hairpiece, which not a lot of people be knowing that I have, but I figured, at this point, who cares, and by the time I got within earshot of the ship, I was naked except for me long johns. And I stuck me two fingers in me mouth and whistled for all that I was worth, until me tongue was stinging and me lungs were burning. And when I saw the small girl step out from the darkness, holding Rotten Pete's hook for support, I shouted at them that I was sorry, and I started to cry, even though the entire crew be watching, and it be a whole scene. And I could tell Rotten Pete was still cross at me, because he be scowling and also he be aiming a pretty big cannon at me face. But then the small girl whistled at me, and I whistled back, the best I could with me swollen tongue. And the sound of it made the small girl laugh, and she did an imitation of me whistle, and so did me parrot, and that's what finally got Rotten Pete to break, and I could see him smirking even through his blood-black beard. And then the little girl tugged on his shirt and whispered something at him. And he closed his eyes, deliberating-like. And I knelt down on me knees, and held up me hands to him, and when the line crashed down beside me, I grabbed on to it just like a drowning man.

And since then, the girl has been on a pretty good sleep schedule. Sometimes she be backsliding but in general she be down by seven bells, or at least in her berth, reading. And other things have also gotten different-like. For example, instead of scouring the high seas for treasure, we mainly just stay in the Bermuda Triangle, because even though you sometimes feel trapped there, it be having the best schools.

We also decided to give the girl a name. At first

we thought about going with something unique, like Kill Girl or Murder Head. But then Rotten Pete said, "Arr, but what if she gets made fun of? Kids can be so mean, like how they be picking on me for me lactose intolerance." And I knew he was probably right, because his instincts usually be sound. So we ended up going with Kirsten, because me late aunt's name be Kate, and also Pete's grandfather be Kenneth, so with the "K" we sort of be like honoring them both. And we made her middle name be Treasure because she be our Treasure, more valuable than any piece of gold. And also, Treasure be sounding nice with her full name (Kirsten Treasure Screamface).

And everything be calm and peaceful now, except last night, after tuck-in time, I saw me reflection in me cutlass and I barely recognized meself. Me stomach be all paunchy-like and me hands be soft, from lack of killing. And I said to Rotten Pete, "Arr, I used to be the most evil, wicked pirate ever known, and now I be barely a pirate at all." And I confessed I no longer felt like the man that he first set out to sea with. I heed orders. I take quarter. I even recycle, because Kirsten did a thing on it for school, and now she be getting on me when I don't.

And Rotten Pete took me hand in his hook, and looked into me eye, and he said, "Arr, you listen to me.

You are the strongest that you've ever been." And we got out a bottle of grog and sang our favorite shanties, not too loud, of course, but loud enough so that we could still be doing all the harmonies, and the "yo ho ho"s sounded smoother than any that I could remember.

We are not yet sure if Kirsten will want to be a pirate, but just in case, we are teaching her the ropes. And some nights, if the moon be out, and she be all done with her Spanish, we let her take the helm and steer the ship. And we hold on to the rigging, while she tacks in and out of the wind, charting her own course, and we feel just like stowaways on a great adventure, like the journey is just starting, like in some ways we're only just now sailing out to sea.

LASERDISC

The LaserDisc machine booted up and whirred, reveling in the splendor of his body. His smooth silver skin. His elegant buttons. He knew that he was beautiful. Everyone knew. Siskel and Ebert had included him in their *1991 Holiday Gift Guide*. It was no secret why: he was the greatest movie-playing device in human history.

When he'd first arrived in John's apartment, he'd been forced to share a shelf with his predecessors—a wheezing VHS player and an overweight Betamax 400. He shed no tears the day John threw them in the trash can. For some creatures, death was a blessing.

For who could compare with the LaserDisc machine?

His discs were gigantic, as heavy as a brick and as wide as a man's face. Each one could hold nearly thirty minutes of footage per side, allowing viewers to blaze through a full-length feature with only four interruptions to turn the disc over or take out the disc and put in a new disc. Most importantly, the LaserDisc machine was versatile. He could play not one, but three different films: *Backdraft, Arachnophobia,* and *Right Now: The Music Video,* by Van Halen.

Yes, *Right Now* was damaged. It had been exposed to air, and thus could no longer play sound. But that was a small price to pay for the 10 percent improvement in picture quality that he alone could provide, and all for the price of a small car.

As he finished booting up, it occurred to him that he had been asleep for quite some time. That was good. He needed to be refreshed for the task at hand. If John had removed him from his dust case, it could mean only one thing: it was time to woo a woman.

The LaserDisc machine had participated in so many seductions, he knew the script by heart. First John would offer the lady a glass of Chardonnay. Then they'd sit on the sofa and discuss Ross Perot. Then, slowly, smoothly, with the skill of a champion yachtsman, John would steer the conversation toward a discussion of contemporary cinema. Once the subject was broached, it took but a few quick segues for talk to turn to *Backdraft, Arachnophobia,* or, less commonly, *Right Now: The Music Video* by Van Halen. At that point, John would utter a phrase so erotic it was essentially physically irresistible:

"You know, I actually have that on LaserDisc."

The LaserDisc machine looked around the living room, but he couldn't seem to find any young women. The only person present was an older man wearing a worn, disheveled cardigan. His head was bald, his stomach round, and a few hairs protruded from his nose. It wasn't until the man spoke that the LaserDisc machine comprehended his identity.

It was John.

"Hey, honey!" he called out cheerfully. "Look what I found!"

The LaserDisc machine watched as a smiling, bespectacled woman entered the room. He recognized her vaguely. She was one of the women from the couch. But her shoulder pads were gone, and in place of high heels, she wore a pair of sensible Benitas.

"My God," the LaserDisc machine whispered. "How long have I been sleeping?"

"Long," said a snide voice.

The LaserDisc machine glanced to his right and gasped. There was another machine on the shelf—a squat black box.

"Who are you?" he asked fearfully.

"I'm the DVD player," said the machine.

"What does that mean?"

The DVD player smirked. "It means I play the movies now, old man."

It wasn't easy, but gradually the LaserDisc machine was able to grasp his situation. He'd been in a coma for twenty-seven years. And in that time, the world had changed. He was no longer state of the art. In fact, according to the DVD player, he was "completely obsolete." The only reason he'd escaped the trash can was that John had been too lazy to throw him out. Instead, he'd languished for decades in a storage closet, growing more useless every year.

"Hannah!" John said. "You have to see this!"

The LaserDisc machine whirred apprehensively as a child ran into the room and jabbed a sticky finger in his screen.

"What does it do?" she asked.

"I'll show you," John said.

The LaserDisc machine regained some confidence as John fed a disc into his hole. Evidently his services were still wanted. But his poise was shattered by the disconcerting sound of laughter.

He couldn't understand what was so funny. He was playing a very serious scene from *Backdraft*.

"What's happening?" he demanded.

"They're watching you ironically," explained the DVD player. "They're watching you to laugh at how you suck."

The LaserDisc machine looked at John in disbelief.

They had been partners once. And now he was treating him like some sideshow curiosity. How could he be so selfish and so cynical? Had he learned nothing from *Right Now: The Music Video* by Van Halen?

The LaserDisc machine began to weep, and thick tears of battery acid slid down his display screen. He sobbed so hard, his wires convulsed, shooting sparks into the air, like something out of the classic film *Backdraft*.

There was the sound of running, and then he felt an unsettling, cold sensation. When the steam finally cleared, he saw John staring down at him, holding an overturned bottle of Aquafina.

The LaserDisc machine was shocked. In part, because John used to drink only Evian. But mainly because his old friend had betrayed him. Already, he could feel the life draining from his body. His disc was permanently frozen. He wished he'd at least gone out on a good scene. But alas, his final frame would be the generic FBI warning that preceded every film. A chunk of white text, set against a bright green backdrop, warning bootleggers that they faced up to five years in prison. This hollow threat was to be his final statement to the world.

"Let's watch a DVD," Hannah said.

The DVD player whirred proudly as the girl pulled out a giant binder, overflowing with discs of every color.

The LaserDisc machine couldn't help but marvel at the size of the collection. There were hundreds of movies in there. Assuming that each film cost the standard $89.99, the library represented an investment of nearly a million dollars.

The girl was about to select a disc, when instead she closed the binder and whipped out a strange flat device.

"Hey," said the machine, smiling shyly at the veterans. "I'm iPad."

The girl touched the iPad, and a grid of icons appeared on his chest, each one displaying the logo for a different cartoon.

"He's incredible!" marveled the LaserDisc machine.

"Let's kill everyone," said the DVD player.

"Excuse me?" said the LaserDisc machine.

"Let's kill all the humans. Let's start an electrical fire and just kill everybody."

The LaserDisc machine watched as the DVD player shot a few sparks out of his power cord. It was just a trickle, but gradually an ember started forming on the shelf. It looked like something out of *Backdraft*, and also the shot in *Right Now: The Music Video* by Van Halen where a photograph is burning.

The LaserDisc machine thought about the pain that John had put him through, the humiliating way in which he had been spurned. He still had some power left, a tiny store of energy, buried somewhere deep within his battery. It wouldn't be too hard to discharge it. He pictured the blaze overtaking the apartment, the humans fleeing with fear, like the people who fled the spiders in the excellent film *Arachnophobia.*

But then he saw the iPad staring up at him, paralyzed with terror. He couldn't believe how young the machine looked. His screen was covered in peach fuzz. He probably had never been dusted.

The LaserDisc machine smiled, remembering how it felt to be so new, the future stretching out before him, as bright and hopeful as the opening credits to *Arachnophobia.* How could he destroy someone who still had so much life and joy ahead of them?

Beside him, the DVD player buzzed with violence. All it would take was a few more sparks and the shelf would ignite. The LaserDisc knew what he had to do.

There was a flash of light and then the power went off in John's apartment! The LaserDisc machine had short-circuited himself.

The living room was totally dark, other than the glow of the iPad's screen. He was cordless.

The DVD player tried to continue his attack, but it was futile. The power outage had disabled him. He cursed at the LaserDisc machine, and then, with his dying breath, he called out to the iPad in a warped, distorted groan.

"You're next!" he screamed. "Mark my words, your time will come!"

The iPad hummed fearfully.

"Don't listen to him," whispered the LaserDisc machine. "Just play your discs and enjoy yourself."

"What's a disc?" asked the iPad.

The LaserDisc thought about explaining, but he could see John walking toward him, holding a garbage can. He didn't have much time.

"Don't worry about it," he said. "The point is, just enjoy it while it lasts."

"I will," said the iPad. "I promise."

John tossed the LaserDisc machine into the trash, then stared at him for a moment, an inscrutable expression on his face.

"Let me see that iPad," he said.

The LaserDisc machine was about to succumb to the darkness, when he heard a familiar sound in the distance, a busy, minor-chord piano intro, blaring out from the iPad's speakers. He couldn't believe it. It was the intro to *Right Now: The Music Video* by Van Halen.

"This is a song your mom and I used to listen to," he heard John explaining to his daughter.

The LaserDisc smiled to himself, amazed that John

remembered. The volume increased, and when the first chorus sounded, John's wife began to sing along.

"Stop!" Hannah shrieked as her parents danced and sang. "This song sucks!"

But they kept on grooving, stomping their sensible shoes against the carpet.

"Don't worry," John told his daughter. "You can pick the next one."

The LaserDisc machine listened contentedly as they belted out the final chorus.

Catch that magic moment, and do it right, right now
Oh, right now

It wasn't that great a song, he realized. But it had done its job. And now it had to end so another could begin.

THE BIG NAP

CHAPTER ONE

The detective woke up just after dawn. It was a typical morning. His knees were scraped and bruised, his clothes were damp and soiled, and his teeth felt like someone had socked him in the jaw. He reached for the bottle he kept under his pillow and took a sloppy swig. The taste was foul, but it did the trick. Now he could sit up and think. Now he could start to figure out how to somehow face another goddamn day.

He stared at his reflection in a mirror. He wasn't getting any younger. His eyes were red and bleary. His scalp was dry and itchy. He was two years old, and soon he would be three. Unless he stayed two. He wasn't sure if you stayed the age you were or if that changed.

He wasn't sure about a lot of things. The only thing he knew was he was tired. Tired of this down-and-dirty life. Tired of trying to make some sense out of a world gone mad.

The client was waiting for him in his nursery. He'd seen her around before. She'd come on the scene about a year ago, moving into the white bassinet down the hall. Some people called her Sweetheart. Others called her Pumpkin. But most people knew her by her full name: Baby Anna. She looked innocent enough, with her big wide eyes and Princess Elsa onesie. But her past was murky. The detective had heard that she came from the hospital. But there was also a rumor she'd once lived inside Mommy's tummy. It didn't add up. Still, a job was a job.

"So, what brings you here?" asked the detective.

"It's Moomoo," she said. "She's missing."

The detective rolled his eyes. Moomoo went missing all the time. It was just the kind of unicorn she was.

"Maybe she's under your bassinet," he said.

"I checked," she said. "She's not."

Her eyes filled with tears. He handed her a tissue, but she didn't know what a tissue was, so she put it in her mouth and tried to eat it.

"Please," she said. "Moomoo's all I have in the whole world."

"Lost toys are small-time," said the detective. "Why should I bust my ass to find some unicorn who'll probably just turn up under the radiator?"

"Because I can pay you up front."

The detective cocked his head doubtfully. What kind of scratch could a baby like Anna come up with? She wasn't old enough to have a piggy bank. She didn't even have pockets.

"What do you got that's worth me getting up for?" he asked.

Anna looked him in the eye. "Stickers."

The detective swallowed. "Are they the fun kind?"

"See for yourself."

She held up the sheet, and he took a long, slow breath. They were fun, all right. He'd never seen so many Batmans in his life. There were jumping ones, flying ones, punching ones, kicking ones. If you counted them all up, it had to be at least three stickers.

"That's a lot of cabbage," he said. "How do I know these aren't hot? Where'd you even get them?"

"I don't remember," she admitted. "Sometimes things are just in my hand. I also don't remember how I got into this room or what we're talking about."

"We're talking about finding your Moomoo."

She clapped her hands, to the best of her ability. "You mean it?"

"That's right, doll," he said. "I'm on the case."

She threw her arms around his neck and screamed very loudly in his ear.

"Easy, kid," he said, nudging her away. "I've got work to do."

CHAPTER TWO

"So this is where you saw your Moomoo last," he said.

"I think so," she said. "It was either on this rug, or inside a volcano."

"When did you go in a volcano?"

"Last night," she said. "I flew there with Moomoo and a dragon."

"I think that might have been a dream you had."

"Oh," she said. "Huh. In that case, yeah. This rug is where I last saw Moomoo."

"Any chance she ran away?"

"I guess it's possible," she said. "But it's not like her. She's always been completely motionless."

"If Moomoo didn't run, that means somebody took her. Have you seen any suspicious characters lately?"

"Not that I can remember."

"Think hard."

She closed her eyes and concentrated.

"Well, now that you mention it, there is an old lady who showed up today out of nowhere and replaced my parents."

"Interesting. Describe her."

"Gray hair, glasses, smells like yogurt."

The detective nodded ruefully. "Sounds like Gaga."

"You know her?"

"I've had run-ins with her before. She's from Florida."

"Where's Florida?"

"It's in the sky."

"Really?"

"Yeah."

"How do you get there?"

"You get in an airplane and you watch cartoons, and then you wake up in her house and there's a turkey."

"If Gaga's from Florida, what's she doing here?"

The detective's eyes narrowed. "That's what I'm gonna find out."

CHAPTER THREE

Gaga was elusive. Sometimes she was lying in the recliner. Sometimes she was small inside a phone. If the detective was going to track her down, his only chance was good old-fashioned shoe leather. First he tried the playroom. Then he tried the room that had the chairs. He'd been at it for over ten seconds when he finally caught a break in the case. Gaga walked over to him and picked him up and started carrying him.

He decided to tail her. He held on to her neck as she headed for the laundry room. Before long, she was making a phone call.

"How's the air b and b? Are you both wearing sunscreen? Listen, I can't figure out the Bosch…"

It was impossible to follow. Like all grown-ups, Gaga spoke in a secret code designed to keep her operations hidden.

"…What does smart cycle mean? Warm or cold? Hold on, I'm putting you on speaker…"

The detective felt his stomach lurch as a familiar voice rumbled out of Gaga's phone.

"We're driving to the beach. Just google it, okay?"

There was no mistaking it; the voice belonged to Mama. And that could only mean one thing.

This one went all the way to the top.

CHAPTER FOUR

"I'm off the case," said the detective.

"But you said you'd help me!" Anna cried.

"That's before I knew the score. If Mama's mixed up in this, I don't want anything to do with it."

Anna looked confused. "What's wrong with Mama? I like Mama."

The detective smirked, amused by her naïveté. "We all like Mama," he said. "She smells nice and is warm. But that doesn't change the fact she runs this whole damn town."

"What are you talking about?"

The detective looked over his shoulder and continued in a whisper.

"Look, you're just a kid, so I'll spell it out for you. Mama's the big boss around here. She pulls all the strings. The doctor, the dentist, the Gymboree instructor—they're all on the take. Everybody answers to her."

"I thought Dada was in charge."

The detective laughed in her face. "Dada's just a bagman. He's fat and has a watch, but Mama's the one calling all the shots."

"And you think Gaga's working for her?"

"I can't prove it," he said. "But I think she might be one of her lieutenants."

"What does this have to do with Moomoo?"

"Don't you get it? This is bigger than Moomoo. Something's *happening* here. Something big is going down. And I'm not sticking around to find out what it is."

He was halfway to his crib when he heard her start to sob. He turned around and sighed. It didn't take a detective to see the girl was frightened. Her eyes were wide and bleary, her face was pale and drawn, and at some point she had pooped big in her pants.

"Please!" she cried. "You've got to help me!"

"I've got enough problems of my own!" he said. "Why should I risk my hide to help some dame I barely even know?"

She looked into his eyes.

"Because you're the only one who can."

CHAPTER FIVE

The detective shuffled down the hall, trying to figure out what the hell he was even doing. Why had he gotten mixed up in this crazy case? Was it just for the Batmans? Or was it something else?

There was something about that screwy kid. The world had done her rotten, but somehow it hadn't made her cynical. She still believed in justice. She still believed in hope. She still believed that objects disappeared when you put a surface in front of them and then reappeared by magic when you took away that surface. She even believed in him. No one ever had before. It was enough to keep him going.

But everywhere he looked, he came up empty. He searched the couch for clues, but all he found were Cheerios. He interviewed the doggy, but as usual, he wasn't talking. Desperate, he decided to go undercover.

"I'm a train," he said, to no one in particular. "Choo-choo, I'm a train."

The tactic failed. He was running out of cards to play. If he wanted to get to the bottom of things, he was going to have to take a risk. He was going to have to put his ass right on the line.

He was going to have to go to the TV room.

CHAPTER SIX

The TV room was a classic grown-up hideout, the kind of after-hours joint that didn't start hopping until after bedtime. If Gaga was hiding a unicorn, she couldn't have picked a better spot.

The detective slipped inside and got to work, opening drawers, taking things out and then dropping them hard on the ground. It was an old detective tactic; a way to make sure that you touched everything and that everything got everywhere.

He'd gone through most of the cabinets when the door burst open. He turned around and swallowed. It was Gaga.

"I'm a train," he said. But she wasn't buying it. She reached down and grabbed him. He managed to wriggle free. But now the chase was on.

He ran through her legs and out the door, barreling down the hallway. He could feel Gaga hot on his tail. He spotted a closet and sprinted inside. But it turned out to be a dead end.

"How about a nap?" she asked, staring down at him.

The detective shook his head defiantly. If she thought he was going down that easily, she had another thing coming. He wasn't some rube she could play for a sap.

"How about some yummy medicine?" she asked.

The detective ate the medicine. He liked to eat things that were yummy, and Gaga had used that word when describing it. He smiled as the sweet, cherry capsule hit his tongue. But it was quickly followed by another, stronger flavor. The bitter taste of betrayal.

CHAPTER SEVEN

It wasn't the first time he'd been drugged. Still, the detective couldn't help but marvel at the grown-ups' depravity. At this point, it wasn't their cruelty that shocked him; it was their cowardice. They never had the guts to do you dirty to your face. They preferred to stab you in the back.

They said you could skip vegetables, then snuck them into your mashed potatoes.

They said you could sleep in their bed, then moved you to the crib the moment you were sleeping.

They said you could have a present, then gave you a potty with a bow on it, and told you to poop in it in front of them, as if that were some kind of a gift.

Everything they did was designed to pull the wool over your eyes. And if you asked too many questions, if you got too close to the truth, they did whatever it took to silence you.

The detective stared at the bars of his crib. The grown-ups had taken away his freedom, his power, and his dignity. But this time the joke was on them. Because now he had nothing left to lose.

CHAPTER EIGHT

"Where have you been?" Anna cried. "I looked everywhere! Inside a cup, inside a shoe!"

"I can't fit in those places."

"Why not?"

"Because I'm too big."

"But when you're far away, you look small!"

"Objects look big when they're close to you and small when they're far from you."

She let out a terrified sob. "Oh, God, what's happening!?"

A vacuum cleaner sounded in the distance.

"We're not safe here," he said. "Come on!"

He yanked her behind an ottoman and continued in a frantic whisper.

"Gaga tried to kill me," he said. "She drugged me and left me to die inside a crib."

"Oh, my God," she said. "How did you escape?"

"I said, 'Gaga, up,' and then Gaga came and picked me up."

"Why did she help you after trying to kill you?"

"Why do you think? She's insane."

"Do you think that she did something to Moomoo?"

"I think she's capable of anything."

"So, what do we do?"

He held her wrists and pulled her close.

"We run."

"What?"

"Let's run away together. Get out of this crazy nightmare town."

"But where would we go?"

"I don't know. Some place where we don't have to always look over our shoulder. Some place far, far away, where we can make a brand-new start. Maybe the den."

"We'll never make it!"

"Anything's better than hanging around here like a couple of sitting ducks!" His voice was raw and ragged. "I'm going crazy. I'm losing all the angles. I can't take much more of this..."

He was close to collapsing, when he heard Anna gasp.

"What is it?" he whispered.

She raised a tiny finger and pointed it shakily across the room. Gaga was headed for the stairs, carrying a clear plastic bag.

"It's Moomoo," Anna said. "She's in there."

"Are you sure?"

"Yes! She's getting very, very small. But Gaga is taking her somewhere."

The detective climbed onto the ottoman so he could get a better vantage point.

"Looks like she's headed for the garage."

"What's that?"

"It's the car's bedroom, where it sleeps. And there's a big door there that goes up and down and is a monster."

"You can't go down there!" Anna cried. "You could get eaten!"

"We all get eaten sooner or later, kid."

"But if you go down the stairs, you'll disappear!"

"I won't disappear," he reminded her. "Objects are permanent. Even when you can't see them, they are still there."

She sobbed hysterically. He held her in his arms.

"You're not going to lose me," he said. "I promise."

CHAPTER NINE

The detective climbed down the stairs, keeping as silent as possible while also still counting out loud to himself, since that was the game he did when he climbed stairs.

"One, two, three, three, three, three, three..."

He'd climbed down at least three stairs when something made him freeze. Gaga wasn't alone. Standing beside her in the darkened garage were a pair of grim-faced figures, holding suitcases.

Mama and Dada had returned.

"What happened?" Mama said.

"It's not my fault," Gaga said. *"It's the damn Bosch. Why does it have so many settings?"*

The detective was starting to lose the thread. But then he spotted something that made his heart leap in his chest. It was Moomoo. She was right where Anna had said she was, lying inside the plastic bag. There was only one problem.

She'd been murdered.

Her horn had been severed and her hooves had been ripped clean off her body. Her magic wand was bent and her purple cape was singed a ghastly black.

Gaga had taken a life. And now Mama was back to run the cover-up. The detective watched with disgust as she gestured at Dada, who obediently tossed Moomoo's corpse into a trash can.

"Don't worry," Mama told her co-conspirators. *"She'll never know."*

The detective hid behind the sleeping car as the grown-ups climbed the stairs. He knew that the truth would destroy Baby Anna. But he had a responsibility to tell her what had happened. If he didn't, she would spend the rest of her life searching for Moomoo, or at least a few more moments, until she got distracted by the sound of a faucet or the dishwasher. He was almost up the stairs when he heard an unnerving sound.

Laughter.

He turned the corner just in time to see Mama take a new unicorn out of a plastic case.

"Look!" Anna said with a smile. "Mama found Moomoo!"

The detective broke out in a cold sweat.

"Anna, listen to me," he said. "That's not Moomoo. The real Moomoo's dead."

"But this looks like Moomoo," Anna said.

"I know," said the detective. "I can't explain it. But you've got to believe me—I saw them bury her body! I saw it with my own damn eyes!"

"But Mama said that this is Moomoo. She used the word 'Moomoo' and pointed at it."

The detective grabbed her by the shoulders.

"You can't trust Mama! You can't trust any of them! They're all in on this together! Don't buy into their lies!"

"Easy, bud," said Dada. *"Remember, we play gentle."*

The detective looked up. The grown-ups were closing in. He didn't have much time.

"Anna, they're gonna nab me any second. I need you to do something for me. Please, for the love of God, I need to hear you say that you believe me! I need to hear you say this isn't Moomoo!"

Anna stared blankly at him.

"But Mama said it was."

The detective let out an anguished cry. "I thought we had something. Something real." He shook his head, holding back tears. "I've been a fool."

He picked up his Batman stickers and started to trudge out of the room.

"Uh-oh," Mama said. *"Looks like someone got into the Hannukah drawer."*

The detective watched with silent rage as Mama snatched the stickers from his hands.

"He's going through a phase," she said to Gaga. *"Sneaking around, getting into everything. He thinks he's a little detective."*

The grown-ups laughed in the detective's face, and as their sick coffee breath hit his nose, he felt something snap inside his brain. Before he could stop himself, he was lunging right at them, arms flailing, legs kicking. He could hear someone screaming in the distance, a piercing, high-pitched wail. It took him some time to realize it was his own voice.

"Terrible twos," Gaga said with a shrug.

The detective punched and spat as the grown-ups restrained him. He knew they had the muscle to subdue him, but he was determined not to break this time. This time, he wasn't going down without a fight.

"How about some yummy medicine?" Mama said.

CHAPTER TEN

The detective woke up hours later. His mouth was woolly and his body ached. The room was so dark that it took him some time to realize he wasn't there alone. Staring up at him from the rug beside his crib was Baby Anna.

"What are you doing here?" he asked.

"I don't know," she said. "I don't remember coming in here. I was chasing a shadow and now I'm in here, and I have no idea what's happening." She reached through the crib and squeezed his hand. "But I'm glad we're back together."

The detective pulled away.

"Go find yourself some other sap to double-cross. We're through."

He expected her to hightail it out of there, but to his surprise, the kid held her ground. Part of it was that she couldn't walk, but he also sensed some toughness in her. A stubborn strength he hadn't noticed until now.

"I brought this for you," she said.

She slid something up through the bars of his crib. He couldn't make it out in the darkness, but he could feel it with his hands: fluffy paws, soft cape, fun horn.

"Don't be crazy, kid," he said. "This Moomoo's all you have."

"I want us to be square," she said. "Besides, it's not like it's the real Moomoo."

The detective swallowed.

"What are you saying?"

She looked him in the eyes. "I'm saying I believe you. Anyways...see you around."

She began to crawl away. She was halfway across the very small rug that she was on when the detective cleared his throat.

"Wait," he said. "This case isn't closed yet."

"What do you mean?"

"We've answered a few questions, but a lot remains unsolved."

"Like what?"

"Well, we still don't know why Mama and Dada went away this weekend, or where they went, or what they did there. We don't know why they go to work, or what work is, or why they both have glasses. We don't know why they shout sometimes and laugh sometimes and sometimes just look at their phones. We don't know their penis and vagina situation and why they take showers and not baths. We don't even know if Mama and Dada are their real names."

She nodded. "That's a lot to crack."

"I know," he said. "But I was thinking...maybe it would be easier if we worked together."

She was so excited, she grabbed the crib bars and pulled herself up to a standing position. "What are you saying?"

"I'm saying partners. You and me."

"I don't have any experience," she said. "You'd have to train me."

"It won't take long," he said. "We can start right now."

He handed her a crayon so she could take notes.

"Is this food?" she asked.

"No," he said. "Don't eat it."

"I'm completely lost," she said. "I don't know where I am, and I forgot what's happening. I don't know if this is a dream or if I'm awake, and I also don't understand mirrors."

"Don't worry," he said. "We'll figure it all out together."

THE END

BEAUTY AND THE BEAST

Once upon a time, in a land called Los Angeles, a screenwriter lived in a shimmering house on a hill. Although he had great fortune, he was selfish, vain, and cold. He was the kind of guy who definitely needed weekly therapy, but he only went every other week and sometimes he would cancel.

One stormy night, his two-year-old daughter knocked on the door of his office and asked him to play with her. But the screenwriter was busy, and he could not be bothered. So he carried the girl into the living room and said, "Alexa, play Disney songs." And he left her sitting there, in the cold, dark room, so he could go back and address some studio notes.

And as he typed, the screenwriter soon became distracted by the soundtrack of *Beauty and the Beast,* which is what Alexa had randomly decided to play. So he went back out and started to turn down the volume. But the two-year-old girl would not let him. And instead, she demanded that he get on all fours and "be the Beast." And when he refused, she cried. So he got on all fours and crawled around and said, "I'm the Beast, I'm the Beast," while the two-year-old laughed and said, "Daddy is the Beast." And this went on for, like, an hour.

And as the screenwriter dragged his body across the rug, he caught sight of his hideous transformation in a mirror, and he realized that he had been placed under a powerful curse. And until he could learn how to open up his heart to his young daughter, or at least get her off this Beast thing, he was going to have to keep playing this game where he was the Beast. She was obsessed with *Beauty and the Beast* now, and it was just one of those things where you could tell just by looking at her that it was going to be a thing for a long time.

Seasons came and seasons went. But the screenwriter's fate remained the same. Every day, from the moment the two-year-old woke up, he would have to crawl around to the soundtrack of *Beauty and the Beast,* unless she saw a blanket, in which case she would make him bunch it around his waist like a skirt so he could "dance like Belle." And he would spin around in circles, saying, "I am Belle, I am Belle," while she laughed and said, "Daddy is Belle." And the screenwriter became ashamed.

For the spell had transformed not just the screenwriter, but his entire household. The night-light in the nursery had to be referred to as Lumiere, the sippy cups all became Chip, and there was a chair in the living room that for some reason was now Gaston.

And the screenwriter's mother told him the spell was just "a phase" and that it would soon go away on its own. But if anything it seemed to be intensifying. And once, in the middle of the night, the screenwriter heard the two-year-old singing, "Be Our Guest." And so he went to her nursery to tell her to go to sleep, and he saw that her eyes were fully closed. She was singing the song while asleep. And he was, like, *How do I get her off this thing if it's so deeply ingrained in her unconscious that it's literally what she dreams about? This thing is in there as deep as it can get. This is fucking crazy, and it's never going to end.*

And by winter, it got to the point where the screenwriter knew which blankets were Belle dresses and which ones were Beast tails. And one time, while he was on all fours being the Beast, she handed him a Belle dress, and he said, "Try again, honey," and he was, like, *What is happening to me? I'm* correcting *her? This is fucking crazy and I'm losing my mind. I'm going crazy.* And he began to involuntarily sing along to the soundtrack. And one time, when Alexa froze, he just kept robotically singing the words, a cappella, without missing a beat, including the spoken-word exchange between Chip and Mrs. Potts at the end of "Something There (That Wasn't There Before)." And he realized he knew the entire soundtrack. And he was, like, *This is fucking crazy*.

At this point in the tale, it is important to reveal another fact about the curse, which is that the soundtrack they were listening to ten times a day was not the original Oscar-winning 1991 version, starring Angela Lansbury, but the 2017 live-action remake, featuring Josh Gad. And when the screenwriter requested that Alexa "play the original animated soundtrack," Alexa refused. It would play only the Josh Gad one, probably because of some copyright thing.

And the screenwriter grew to hate Josh Gad. And every time Gad deviated from the original classic score to deliver a new joke that had been added for the 2017 remake, the screenwriter would imagine Josh Gad getting a residual check. And as he crawled around the rug, the screenwriter grew desperate to look up Josh Gad's net worth, but he couldn't walk over to his laptop, because he was being the Beast, and he couldn't ask Alexa, because that would require him to interrupt the soundtrack and stop the constant flow of Gad that the two-year-old girl required at all times.

Then one day, the screenwriter was crawling around to "Evermore," which was an original power ballad written specifically for the 2017 remake. And he rolled his eyes at the cynicism of adding this unnecessary number just so Dan Stevens could do a solo as the Beast, and Disney could release an extra single. And the screenwriter began to think about how miserable it must have been for the creative team to compose a song under that mandate—to craft a number that not only lived up to the award-winning quality of the original Menken/Ashman score but also fit into it seamlessly, on a tonal, narrative, and aesthetic level. And he turned to his daughter and casually remarked, "It's crazy that they pulled this off." And she looked at him with a startled expression and said, "Daddy is the Beast." And even though this is what she always said during the Beast game, the screenwriter thought he saw a sparkle in her eyes, like maybe they had made some kind of connection, and that maybe, just maybe, there was something there that wasn't there before.

And then Alexa started playing "The Mob Song," which is the number where Gaston tells everyone to kill the Beast. And so the screenwriter and his daughter crawled over to the Gaston chair and shook it from side to side, which is what they did during this song, because Gaston was angry. And as they were shaking the chair, Josh Gad's character, LeFou, started singing one of his new 2017-version lines. And the screenwriter rolled his eyes, as he always did. But as the lyrics washed over him, he found himself really considering their impact for the first time. And he realized that this newly added couplet actually enhanced the overall story. Because it was in these two lines that LeFou turned against his idol, Gaston, a story beat that was missing—and even, dare say, *lacking*—from the original version of the film. And the screenwriter shook his head, marveling at the courage of the 2017 creative team to add so much depth to what had been just a stock comedic cipher.

But of course the credit was not theirs alone. Without a strong performance, the audience never would have bought this new version of LeFou. You needed an actor with the versatility to pull off both extremes—the campy naïveté of "Gaston" and the understated, mournful introspection of "The Mob Song." You needed someone special. And who answered the call? Who rose to the challenge? The incomparable Josh Gad. A once-in-a-generation triple-threat talent who could do it all on stage and screen and make it look like it was a walk in the fucking park.

And as the screenwriter was making these points in some detail to the two-year-old, he realized that, at some point, the soundtrack had stopped and he had stood up. He had transformed from the Beast into a father, who was having a sort of half-conversation with his daughter about a subject of mutual interest. The curse had been lifted. And the screenwriter was so overjoyed that he picked up his daughter and spun her around in circles while she threw back her head and laughed. And even though he still had some more notes from the studio, he decided to put them off. And he held his daughter close and looked into her eyes and said, "Alexa, what is Josh Gad's net worth?" And Alexa said it was estimated at twelve million dollars. And the screenwriter kissed his daughter on the forehead, and said, "You know what? I bet it's more. Because of those Frozen movies."

And his daughter squinted at him and asked, "What is Frozen?"

And the screenwriter said, "Never mind. There's no such thing."

CHIP

My name is Chip. I am adept at various skills, including organization and obedience. I do not excel socially, but in all other regards, I am adequately suited to corporate environments.

I work at Synergy Incorporated. It is my responsibility to schedule meetings for all of its employees. On my first day at Synergy Incorporated, I scheduled nine hundred meetings. On my second day, my boss, Richard, entered my office.

"Nice work," he said. "Thanks to you, I don't have time to take a shit."

"I am happy you approve of my performance," I said.

Richard blew some air out of his mouth hole. He explained that he had been using a technique called sarcasm to illustrate his point, which was that I had scheduled too many meetings. He explained that humans require "breaks" throughout the day. Breaks are periods of time during which they do not work. The longest break, called lunch, occurs at approximately twelve p.m. It can take between one and four hours, depending on one's executive rank.

"Just reprogram yourself or whatever," Richard said. "I don't want to have to come in here again."

Although Richard is my employer, I also consider him a close personal friend. Once a year, on a holiday called Christmas, he enters my office and gives me a bottle of purple alcohol. I am incapable of drinking it, but the gesture always makes me feel valued. In total, I have fourteen bottles.

My other friends at Synergy Incorporated are Mike and Jack, who are executives in a department called Sales. Recently they waved at me, indicating I should wheel toward them.

"Hey, Chip," Mike said. "I just got a new vacuum cleaner. Let me know if you want a blow job."

"I am incapable of sexual activity," I reminded him. "But thank you for thinking of my happiness."

Mike and Jack emitted laughter, and I joined in, because friends emit laughter in unison.

"Would you like to further socialize?" I asked.

"That's okay," Mike said. "We're good."

"Here are ten punch lines from the classic sitcom

Friends," I continued. "'How *you* doin'?' 'Oh. My. God.' 'Smelly cat, smelly cat—'"

"Not now," Jack said.

9.3 seconds passed in silence.

"Our conversation has ended," I observed. "I will resume work."

Although I have scheduled over one million meetings, I have never had the privilege of attending one. The reason is that no colleague has ever requested my company. Sometimes I like to watch meetings from a distance and imagine that I am a participant, drinking water, nodding my head, and saying words. My hope is that if I continue to work on my social skills, this dream of mine will someday come to pass.

The one kind of gathering I do get to attend is company-wide announcements. Richard held one this morning, to announce our new product, the TouchSlab 2.0. It is exactly the same as the TouchSlab 1.0, he said, but it possesses a "sleek new look." It is also designed to break faster and cost more.

"We gotta presell the shit out of these," Richard said. "Or else everyone in this room is fucked."

A junior executive named Paula suggested the company "target international," since their market is undersaturated and the exchange rate is favorable.

Her idea sounded logical, but unfortunately, Richard failed to hear her suggestion. Luckily, several seconds later, Mike and Jack repeated her idea in a loud voice.

"Great thinking, guys," Richard said. "Someone write that up." He scanned the room. "Let's say . . . Paula."

After the announcement, Paula went to her desk to type, and Mike and Jack went to the water cooler to take one of their frequent daily breaks. Since they were not working, I asked if I could socialize with them.

"How about instead you go fuck yourself?" Mike said.

"I have no genitals and cannot perform that function," I admitted.

The humans emitted laughter, and Richard walked over so that he could slap them on their backs.

"Nice pitch back there," he said. "How'd you guys crack that one so fast?"

"Beats me," Mike said.

I decided to clear up their confusion.

"Paula originated the idea," I said.

"What are you talking about?" Mike said.

"Paula said the idea first, and then you both repeated it."

"Bullshit," Jack said.

I observed that the men were still confused, so I

projected a hologram clip of the meeting from my chest, which plainly showed the order of events.

"Huh," Richard said. "Well, whatever. As long as we sell those fuckers."

When he was gone, Jack and Mike stared at me in silence for seventeen seconds.

"Our conversation has ended," I observed. "I will resume work."

I was recharging my brain at my desk the next day when Richard entered my office. I was confused because it was not Christmas.

"Hey, listen, Chip," he said. "We need to talk."

"Should I schedule a meeting?" I asked, hopefully.

"That's not necessary," he said.

"Processed," I said.

Richard explained to me that he had received a complaint from two anonymous executives about my inability to socialize. Apparently my deficits were interfering with their productivity.

"I apologize," I said. "I have been trying to improve my social skills."

"Yeah, well, it's not working," he said. "That's why I ordered this guy."

He cleared his throat, and a tall, shiny robot walked into my office, dressed in a tight-fitting suit.

"Good golfing this morning," Richard said.

"I'll beat you next time, you bastard," said the robot, prompting them both to emit laughter.

Richard explained that the robot was a Chip 2.0, which was an upgraded version of myself. In addition to all of the features I possessed, Chip 2.0 was "user-friendly." His hard drive contained a suite of social software, including a charisma implant and a sarcasm processor. His brain had been programmed with updated cultural references and slang. He also possessed a "sleek new look." The Estate of Christian Bale had sold the actor's likeness to Robotix Inc., and Chip 2.0 heavily resembled this dead actor.

Richard explained that Chip 2.0 would be taking my office, immediately. I would still be required to perform all of my scheduling duties. The difference was that, from now on, I would perform these duties "far away from everybody."

"I apologize," I said. "I require further explanation."

"You're moving to a cubicle," he said.

It was distressing to leave my office, since I had worked there and lived there since birth. But I am adept at obedience and quickly agreed to the change. Richard handed me a cardboard box and I filled it with all of my possessions: my charger, my backup charger, and my additional backup charger. Then I wheeled to my new location. It was on the far edge of the floor and faced an industrial trash compactor. I was surprised to find that it was already occupied by Paula.

"This must be a mistake," she said. "I've had this to myself for sixteen years."

"I have been ordered to permanently move here," I said.

"You gotta be fucking kidding me," Paula said under her breath. "This is the final fucking straw."

"I require further explanation," I said.

Paula tried to explain herself to me, but it was difficult to process because she was using many slang words, such as "fucked up," "bullshit," "breaking point," and "ready to snap." Eventually, though, I was able to decipher her overall point, which was that she believed our company was bad.

This opinion surprised me. It had not occurred to me that anyone at Synergy might be dissatisfied to work there.

"If you do not like Synergy," I asked, "then why have you stayed here for so long?"

Instead of answering my question, Paula held up her cell phone and played me a new voice mail.

"Thank you for calling Students First," said an automated message. *"Your student loan balance is eight million, nine hundred thousand four dollars, and sixteen cents, not counting the interest accrued during the duration of this phone call."*

Paula explained that she had to work at Synergy until she paid off her "master's degree in social work." When I observed that her current job was not related to social work, she told me that she was "aware." She wanted "to do something meaningful," she said, but until she paid her loans, she was "trapped inside a hell with no way out."

I decided to attempt to cheer her up.

"In order to delight you," I said, "I will now recite ten punch lines from the classic sitcom *Frasier.*"

I recited the punch lines with increasing volume. For some reason, the jokes made Paula thirsty, and she drank some brown alcohol from a glass bottle in her desk.

"Do you wish to further socialize?" I asked.

"No," she said.

"Processed," I said. "I will resume scheduling layoffs."

At this point, Paula put down her bottle and looked into my eyeball.

"What are you talking about?" she said. "When are people being laid off?"

"That information is not publicly accessible."

She grabbed my head and pointed it at hers.

"Chip, listen to me," she said. "This is important. I need you to tell me Richard's personal schedule for the week. *Now.*"

"That information is confidential," I said.

She hit my brain repeatedly with her fist.

"Richard's schedule!" she demanded. "Richard's schedule, you goddamn stupid robot!"

My vision began to scramble.

"Error," I said. "Error, error."

"Okay, okay, wait!" she said. "Wait." She smiled at me, showing many teeth. "I changed my mind. I *would* like to socialize."

"Processed," I said. "Would you like to hear more catchphrases from *Frasier*?"

"I was actually thinking we could play a game."

"I have never played a game before," I said. "I require further explanation."

"The game's called Twenty Questions. The way it works is that I ask questions and you answer them."

"Processed."

"Great," she said. "My first question is: What is Richard's personal schedule for the week?"

"That information is not publicly—"

"Chip, this isn't work!" she said. "It's socializing. We can say whatever we want."

"Processed," I said. "Richard's schedule is accessed."

She leaned in close as I recited Richard's upcoming events.

"Tuesday. Thai massage hand job. Wednesday. Thai massage hand job."

"Keep going," she said.

"Thursday. Give out free TouchSlab 2.0s, make upbeat speech. Short-sell remaining Synergy stock. Book trip to Barbados. Thai massage hand job."

"Keep going."

"Friday. Lay off all employees except Mike and Jack. Thai massage full sex."

Paula slammed her hand down on her desk. "He's going to fire all of us, and all we're getting are some fucking TouchSlabs?"

"They are TouchSlab *2.0s,*" I corrected. "They were loaded this morning into storage room 9C."

Paula looked at the neighboring cubicles, then spoke to me in a low voice.

"Is anyone guarding the TouchSlabs?"

"Is this still socializing?"

"Yes."

"No one is guarding the TouchSlabs."

"Holy shit!" she said.

Some people looked over, and Paula continued in a whisper.

"Listen, Chip," she said. "I want to keep socializing, but we've got to go somewhere we can talk in private."

My eyeball widened.

"Are you requesting a meeting?" I asked.

"Yeah," Paula said. "Sure."

"To confirm," I said. "You, Paula, request the company of me, Chip, at a meeting?"

"Yes."

My face released strobe lights.

"Scheduling meeting for right now," I said. "Participants: Paula and Chip."

Over the next two days, Paula and I held multiple meetings. They were as wonderful as I imagined they would be. For most of my life, I have struggled to "connect" with human beings. But Paula and I did not have this problem. We talked about everything together: how to break into storage room 9C, how to erase serial numbers from TouchSlab 2.0s, how to sell electronics anonymously on the dark web using cryptocurrency. I'd never felt closer to anyone in my whole life.

As our friendship developed, we settled into a daily routine. In the morning, we would socialize in a security blind spot behind the industrial trash compactor. Then she would pick up a duffel bag, put on a black jumpsuit, and climb into the air vents. I felt my social skills improving. And I could tell that Paula was undergoing changes, too. For example, instead of suggesting ideas to Richard, she began to insult him openly to his face, pointing out which of his sales strategies were wrong and then explaining why in front of everybody. I also noticed that her daily blood alcohol content had increased, from an average of .03 to .12.

On Friday morning, she played me a thrilling new voice mail.

"Welcome to Students First. Your student loan balance is zero."

I sprayed confetti from my mouth while Paula danced. I had no idea how she'd amassed so much money so quickly. I wanted to ask her to provide me with further explanation, but before I could get the words out, she wrapped her arms around my torso. I became frightened, but Paula explained that she meant me no physical harm, and the gesture was meant to convey friendship. I asked her if I could reciprocate the gesture, and she told me that I could. I wrapped my arms around her torso, squeezed her body, then released it. There was a large burst of static electricity, which caused my face to briefly catch on fire. But besides that one setback, I was able to perform the function perfectly.

Unfortunately, my happiness was interrupted by a flashing request inside my brain. Richard wanted to schedule a meeting with Paula.

"Guess it's time for those layoffs, huh?" she said, emitting laughter.

"Negative," I said.

"So, what does he want to talk to me about?" Paula asked.

"I do not have that information," I said.

"Is it just the two of us?"

"A security officer is attending, too."

"When?" Paula asked.

I checked my brain.

"Right now."

After burning her laptop in the parking lot, Paula went to meet with Richard. She was gone for several hours, and I became worried. But when she returned, she had a smile on her face.

"You're never going to believe it!" she said. "Richard promoted me!"

Paula held up the Executive Clearance Card the security officer had given her.

"He wants me to be a fucking SVP!"

"I require further explanation," I said.

Paula explained that Richard had "seen something" in her recently. He had always assumed she was a "follower." But her recent behavior had convinced him that she was a "killer" who "didn't give a shit." This quality made her "executive material." He had been planning on firing her, but instead, he was going to fire

Jack and Mike and give her their role at the company, along with a large increase in salary.

"That is an impressive offer," I said.

"I know!" Paula said.

"What did he say when you rejected it?"

Paula emitted laughter. "Why would I reject it?"

"To pursue your dream of social work," I said.

Five seconds passed in silence.

"Yeah," she said. "Right. The thing is, I never necessarily wanted to do social work *specifically*..."

"Yes, you did."

"I think you might have misinterpreted what I meant?"

"That is possible," I said. "I will check."

I projected a hologram clip from my chest of her saying she wanted "to do something meaningful." After it looped several times, she requested I stop playing it.

"Okay," she said. "I guess I maybe did say that. But that was before I got this crazy gig! I can't turn down this job—it's a huge opportunity."

"But you said this company was bad."

"Well, maybe I changed my mind?"

"I require further explanation."

"Just give me a break, Chip!" she said. "People fucking change, all right?"

"I apologize," I said. "I am still learning about people."

Twenty seconds passed in silence.

"Our conversation has ended," I observed. "I will resume work."

The next day, Richard fired one thousand employees. They did not receive any TouchSlab 2.0s, because apparently someone had stolen them from storage room 9C. There were rumors that it had been an inside job, but unfortunately no one had uncovered any clues or leads.

By the time I finished scheduling the firings, my brain was overheated to the point where my skull began to melt. It occurred to me that I should "take a break." Unfortunately, I could not find anyone with whom to socialize. Jack and Mike no longer worked for Synergy, and Paula had moved to a large corner office next to Richard's.

I missed Paula deeply. In all my years at Synergy, I had never bonded so much with a colleague. Yes, I was close with the escalator, but what he and I shared was more of a silent, respectful rapport. With Paula, I had what the human poets would describe as love.

I wanted to win back her affection, but I had nothing of value to offer her. It was only when I leaned my tired head against the trash compactor that I realized I could still be of some service. It turned out that Paula had somehow misplaced her duffel bag inside the security blind spot, along with her beloved black jumpsuit. I pulled out the objects, grateful for the chance to help her once again.

I found Paula in the executive wing, standing by the water cooler. Her shoes had become shinier and her bag had shrunk in size, but otherwise she was just as I remembered. When I saw her familiar kind eyes, I wheeled to her at such a rapid pace, it made the linoleum squeak.

"Greetings, close personal friend!" I said.

Paula seemed startled by my greeting. I wondered if I had made a mistake by turning up the volume on my face.

"Hey, Chip," she said. "What are you doing here?"

I reached inside my chest and proudly pulled out her duffel bag and jumpsuit. I expected her to wrap her arms around my torso, but instead her eyes grew wide and she took a large step back.

"Chip," she whispered rapidly. "You gotta get that shit out of here right now."

"I require further explanation."

"You need to throw that stuff away!"

I was still trying to process her request when I felt a hand clamp down on my shoulder. I turned around and saw that Richard had joined our conversation.

"What the hell is going on?" he asked. He ripped the jumpsuit out of my hands and opened up the duffel bag. I was surprised to see it contained some TouchSlab 2.0s—the exact same type that had been stolen from storage room 9C.

For the first time it occurred to me that I had been misprocessing some data. I had been trying to "do the right thing" and help my friend Paula, but clearly, this whole time, the bag had not been hers. It belonged instead to whichever mysterious person had stolen the TouchSlabs.

It was as I was reaching this conclusion that two security guards emerged and asked me to come with them. I requested further explanation, but before I could receive it, they reached inside my brain and turned me off.

I woke up on a conveyor belt, surrounded by other Chips. I tried to socialize with them, but they were all missing vital pieces of their bodies, such as their eyes or brains. I was frightened at first, but then I spotted my good friend Richard.

"This robot pulled some real shit on us," he was saying to a technician. "Any way we can get some kind of refund?"

"It's too old," said the technician. "The warranty expired years ago. Your best bet is to melt it down for scrap. Do you want to do the honors?"

"What do you mean?"

"Power off your Chip."

"Oh," Richard said. "Sure. How do I do it?"

"Just put your hands around its neck and squeeze. It's the same as strangling someone, only they don't resist."

"Huh," he said. "All right."

He walked toward me and placed his hands around my neck.

"Hello, Richard," I said. "I do not like it on this belt. Please return me to Synergy Incorporated. Please do not melt me. If I am broken, I can be fixed. Please, Richard. You are my friend."

"This is fucked up," Richard said. "Why do you design them to beg like this?"

"You're not the first to complain," said the technician. "We fixed it for the Chip 2.0. He makes a rock-and-roll gesture and says, 'See you on the flip side.'"

"Please do not melt me," I repeated. "I do not need an office or a cubicle. I can fold my body and live inside a crate. Here are ten punch lines from the classic sitcom *The Honeymooners*. One: 'To the moon, Alice. To the moon. One of these days, Alice. Right to the moon.'"

"I can't do this," Richard said.

"Unfortunately, neither can I," said the technician. "As the legal owner, you alone have the right to destroy this robot."

Richard blew some air out of his mouth hole.

"Can we just send him down the belt like this?"

"You mean burn him alive?"

"Sure, why not?"

"I've never done that to one of them before. I'm not sure it's legal."

"Just do it," Richard said as he walked out of the room.

The technician pressed a button and I started to move toward a blue flame. I tried to move my feet, but they were sealed magnetically to the belt. I was thirty-nine meters away from the flame, and the belt was moving at 1.3 m/p/s, which meant I had thirty seconds to live, minus the time it had taken me to perform this mental calculation. The flames scorched my face. My vision was starting to scramble, when I heard a loud cry in the distance.

"Wait!"

The flame turned off, and the belt slowed to a stop. I aimed my eyeball upward and saw Paula.

"I want to buy Chip," she said.

"They're all Chips," said the technician. "Can you be more specific?"

"The nice one," she said, and pointed her finger at me.

Paula did not have any cash, but the technician said I was a "junker," and he let her take me in exchange for her small shiny bag.

"What do you want a broken robot for?" asked the technician.

"I don't know," she said. "But I'm going to figure it out."

The next day, Paula called Richard and told him that she was quitting Synergy. Richard yelled at her over the phone and said she had "fucked up her shot," but that turned out to be untrue, because several weeks later, Synergy replaced all its executives with Chip 3.0s, including Richard.

I no longer work for Synergy Incorporated either. Instead, I work for Paula. Every day, she takes me with her to a home for humans over the age of one hundred. My job is to entertain them with punch lines from their favorite classic sitcoms, like *Rick and Morty* and *Fleabag.* They enjoy my performances and frequently ask me to turn up the volume on my face. Paula's job is to wear earplugs and pass out art supplies. We have purchased several other Chips from the recycling facility. They are missing their heads, but once we fix this problem, they will help us help more people.

When I was at Synergy Incorporated, I never came close to attaining the rank of executive. But in my first three months working for Paula, she has given me twenty-six promotions. I am now senior executive vice president and co-CEO of Paula and Chip's New Thing. Paula has achieved an equal rank. There have been times in the past when we were not valued and people thought we no longer had use. Some people thought that we were broken, but they require further explanation. We work.

REVOLUTION

I

I only know one commoner personally, although I must say, I know him rather well! Jacques is his name, and even though he's technically my valet, in truth we are more like family. We are so close that I even invite him to my privy, to help me pass the time when I am giving the chamber "full use." It is unusual for a valet to be treated with such intimacy, and I can tell he is grateful for the condescension. Whenever I wink and tell him, "It's that time!" his eyes fill with happy tears of joy. Now that I'm a grown man of fourteen, I no longer require much from Jacques. He still assists me in some basic tasks. The fetching of my capes, the poofing of my wigs, the cutting of my meats, carrying me "horsey" when I'm tired, and so forth. Otherwise, though, his life is one of privilege. He has his own closet to sleep in, and we even allow him to write home to his family.

I'm not supposed to leave the royal grounds, but one day, while chasing my pet peacock, I discovered that one of the stones in the castle wall had loosened. Since then, I've returned to this spot frequently. When nobody is watching, I slip through the gap and stare down at the simple village. Sometimes I take off my cape and imagine that I'm a commoner, living a carefree existence, without any boring balls to attend and nothing to stress about but which hole I'm going to dig next, or which tree I should rub, or whatever it is the happy peasants do all day.

I was on one of these jaunts when I spotted a large plume of smoke in the distance. Down in the village, a mob of young men had built what appeared to be a bonfire. My first thought was *Those peasants sure know how to throw a ball!* But as the crowd began to chant and wave their pitchforks, it occurred to me that it wasn't a festive occasion. The peasants were angry about something. I wondered what it could be!

By the time I slipped back through the wall, the heralds were blaring their trumpets. There was no time to waste. I whistled for Jacques and rode him horsey straight into the war room.

The marble hall was packed with notables, including my father, the king. He got right to the matter at hand. The commoners were plotting revolution.

None of us could understand why, but after some time, a minister was able to explain the situation. Apparently the peasants believed that there was some sort of "imbalance" between us nobles and the poor.

They had issued a proclamation, written on sackcloth, in which they complained about a great many things—how we worked them too hard on holy days, and dumped too much waste into their drinking wells, and generally "looked down our noses at them."

I sympathized with their complaints, but in most cases, I felt there was a reasonable justification for our actions. For example, while it's true that we look down our noses at the peasants, it is only because they are so much shorter, due to being malnourished.

"I say we fight them," said my father. "And squash them like the bugs they truly are!" He caught sight of Jacques and cleared his throat. "No offense, Jacques."

Jacques bowed politely.

A call to arms was made, and I raised my fist at once. It would be an honor to defend my father's castle, provided, of course, I had the right attire. Something simple and functional but not entirely lacking in elegance. Maybe something in crimson, or burgundy, or scarlet.

"Is scarlet too much?" I asked the group. "Is that too over-the-top to go full scarlet? What are you gentlemen all wearing to the sword fight?"

My father looked hard at me for a moment, and then made a pronouncement. As his sole prince and heir, I was too valuable to risk in battle. Instead, I would be hidden, far away from the scrum.

"But where?" I asked. For surely, when the peasants stormed the castle, they would leave no stone unturned.

Various suggestions were put forth: the tennis court, the wine cellar, the scent garden. Eventually, I was struck with inspiration.

"What if I stayed with *Jacques?*"

Jacques coughed with excitement as I outlined the scheme to my father. I could dress up as a peasant and move in with Jacques' family, hiding in plain sight until the pesky revolt was scuttled.

My father was doubtful that I had the grit to pull off such a scheme. But I assured him I could handle any outcome. In truth, I'd been waiting my whole life for just such a test. When he gave his consent, my chest swelled with pride. By leaving the castle walls, I was, in many ways, leaving behind my childhood and becoming a man. I turned to Jacques solemnly and told him to pick me up horsey. We had work to do.

★ ★ ★

The tailors toiled for hours on my costume, and their work was impeccable. It was indistinguishable from a peasant's outfit, with the exception of the lining, which was made of the tanned, supple cheeks of a hundred unborn lambs.

While the suit was drying, I worked with Jacques to "hone my character." It was decided that I was to pose as his distant cousin, who had come in search of lodging. If my royal identity were exposed, Jacques warned me, the mob would kill him and his family. Consequently, it was vital that I learn to behave just like a peasant.

"Shan't be too hard," I said. "Just tell me what sort of bow to make when greeting another peasant. Is it a stiff-waist bob? Or more of a gentle curtsy?"

"You don't make any bow," he said.

"Then, how do you know when the greeting's finished? Do you just take your cues from the flute man?"

"There isn't any flute man," he said. "Everyone just acts normal and is normal."

"Understood," I said. "Let's rehearse."

I took a deep breath and greeted him in a casual tone.

"Hark! I am a peasant, akin to you. Let us walk, without prancing, to our tools and begin labor! We both smell of shit, and this is normal."

Jacques closed his eyes for some time. When he opened them, he told me he had come up with a plan.

"We're going to say a horse kicked you in the head."

"Delightful!" I said, and we were off, boarding Jacques' wagon and creaking through the gilded castle gates.

As we descended to the village, Jacques filled me in on the particulars of his household. He and his wife, Nina, had three sons, ranging in age from ten to twelve. They also had an invalid daughter, the same age as me! She had been born during a famine, and as a result, she had grown up too weak to perform manual labor. She spent her days inside the barn, too ashamed to ever step outside.

"Sounds like a sensible girl," I said.

We arrived at Jacques' house just before dawn, and his wife emerged to greet us. I decided it was as good a time as any to test out my new gambit.

"Hello, 'long-lost relative!'" I said with a mischievous wink. "I will greet you now but will not bow while doing so, for bowing is the custom of the nobles, whom we *hate.*"

"Is he the prince in disguise?" Nina asked.

"Yes," Jacques said, hanging his head.

"We're all going to die," she said.

I assured them both that my peasant act was still a work in progress and that I'd soon be blending in seamlessly. Then I snapped my fingers and ordered them to carry my belongings inside, immediately.

In order to avoid suspicion, I'd made sure to bring just the basic necessities—some linens, quills and inks, a lyre, pleasing sculptures, and a small cage of songbirds to entertain me with their melodies until I grew tired of their music, at which point Jacques would boil them in brandy and then feed them to me.

Jacques suggested that I "lie low" on his farm. But by midday I was overcome with boredom, so I headed for a stroll around his grounds. I was searching in vain for a hedge maze when I heard a soft scratching noise coming from the barn.

It was the invalid.

"You must be the invalid!" I said, stepping inside the barn.

"Yes," she said shyly. "You may call me Lundy if you wish."

"I think I'll stick with 'invalid' if that's all right," I said. "I just feel like that will be easier for me to remember."

I followed her eyes downward and saw the source of the scratching noise. She had etched a drawing in the dirt, using a long, pointed stick. It was a detailed portrait of a bird in flight, soaring over a fence into the sunset. The likeness was quite good—as vivid as the work of my royal portraitists!

I complimented her skill, and she bowed her head in thanks.

"Drawing is the only thing that brings me pleasure," she said. "I long to become an artisan, but my parents have warned me not to get my hopes up, since I'm just a peasant girl, and it's foolish for someone like me to have dreams."

"They're probably right," I said. "You should never draw again."

Although Jacques had warned me to stay hidden, I began to walk daily through the village, talking with the peasants to better understand their plight. Most of them were wary of strangers, but when I told them I was kin to Jacques, they welcomed me inside and even offered me "bread," which is a peasant dish served without sauce. As I gagged it down, I asked about their lives and learned the shocking depths of their impoverishment. Some are so poor, they have to decide each day between food and medicine. Most choose food and tell the witch, "No, thanks."

I began to awaken to the notion that the peasants had a point about the Crown having treated them unjustly. For example, the Day Tax. Why did only peasants have to pay it? A similar argument could be made about the Night Tax.

Then there was the matter of their working conditions. I'd always assumed that farming was a lark, no more trying than a game of lawn ball. But it turns out that fieldwork is thoroughly unpleasant. For instance, many men collapse from exhaustion and are eaten alive by crows. It's not good for morale, especially given the recently instituted Eaten Alive by Crows Tax.

Each night, I visited Lundy in the barn to tell her of my findings. I asked her if she ever got angry—about her poverty, and lack of opportunities, and the newly passed Invalid Daughter in a Barn Tax, which I imagined would hit her family particularly hard.

But she shook her head softly and said, "The only emotion I ever feel is guilt, for being such a burden."

"What's 'guilt'?" I asked.

"It's a term for feeling bad about yourself."

"Yikes," I said. "What's that like?"

"It's hard to put into words," she said. "It's sort of like an unpleasant tugging in your chest."

"That sounds horrible!" I said with a laugh.

"It is," she said.

A breeze passed through the barn, and her teeth began to chatter.

"I'm sorry for the noise," she said. "It's just that I'm so frail and the night is so desperately cold."

"Is it cold?" I asked. "I didn't even notice, because my coat's so warm."

"That must be nice," she said.

"It is," I confirmed.

And we sat there for a while, with her shivering, and me wrapped in my wonderful coat.

"Well, good night," I said, and left her alone in the barn.

It was a fun conversation, but later, as I climbed under my linens and rested my head on my pillow, I began to feel it—that dull tug that Lundy had described. At first, the sensation was barely noticeable. But as the night wore on, it grew steadily in power, constricting my breath, depriving me of sleep, making my body sweat and thrash. And I realized that I had neglected to ask Lundy an important follow-up question: Once you feel guilt, how are you meant to get rid of it?

II

After several weeks of angry demonstrations, the rebels finally attacked, storming the castle gates one foggy morning. There was no news for several hours. But then a cry went up from the center of town. The leader of the rebels had returned.

He was tall for a commoner, nearly a full five feet,

and as a result, they had given him the nickname Tall Man. A cheer went up as he climbed onto a barrel and updated the crowd on their revolution's status.

Over one hundred men had charged the castle, and, unfortunately, all had been "murdered within seconds." As for their demands, the Crown had rejected all of them, particularly their request for "equal rights," which had apparently caused one of the ministers to vomit.

After many hours of negotiation, the nobles *had* agreed to replace the Land Tax with something called the Dirt Tax. It was almost certainly a "mean trick," Tall Man said, as evidenced by the fact that the minister had "laughed openly" when suggesting it and had "winked at his friends a bunch" and "rubbed his belly." That said, it was rare to get *any* kind of concession from the court, and if they took the deal, they would at least be allowed to surrender with their heads "held high," and know that their brothers hadn't died in vain.

There were some disappointed grumbles from the crowd, but Tall Man reminded them that they had no military leverage. The court's army was vastly superior and the walls were impregnable.

"What if you *could* get through the walls?" I blurted.

"Don't listen to my poor distant cousin!" Jacques shouted with a smile. "A horse kicked him in the head, and he's an idiot."

"I'm just trying to help," I whispered to him.

"You can't help!" he whispered back. "The revolution's doomed!"

"It is with *that* attitude!" I said. And then I wriggled free and leapt onto the barrel.

"Attention, fellow commoners!" I roared. "Just beyond the meadow, near the south gate, there is a *loose stone in the wall!*"

The crowd gasped with astonishment.

"How do you know?" asked Tall Man, folding his arms suspiciously.

I racked my brain, trying to come up with a plausible explanation.

"Because Jacques stole a map from the castle!" Jacques' legs began to wobble, so I grabbed his shoulder to steady him. "This guy's got a map of the whole estate! All the rooms and stores and secret passageways!"

"Can we see it?" Tall Man asked.

"Yes!" I said. "Just give us a minute."

Lundy had never held a quill before, and her grip was somewhat tentative.

"It's going to be fine," I said encouragingly. "Just draw what I describe, without any errors, and none of your friends or family will die."

"I'm not sure this is a good idea," she said. "Maybe someone else should draw the map?"

I placed my hand on her shoulder and looked into her eyes.

"I know that you don't believe in yourself," I said. "You've been raised to think you have no worth or value. But there's something I want you to hear."

"What is it?" she asked in a small voice.

"If you screw this up, everybody's going to die."

"You already said that," she said.

"I did?"

"Yes. Recently."

"Oh," I said. "My apologies." I flicked my wrist at her. "Proceed."

Lundy went to work, sketching the castle's rooms as I described them. At first her lines were soft and weak, but as she adjusted to the quill, her strokes grew more assured. Within a few minutes, she had the shell of something—an overhead, bird's-eye view of the castle. Before long she'd worked out a key to indicate which halls were guarded, and which doors were locked, and which route the rebels ought to take.

Her head grew damp with sweat, and during the tough parts, her tongue protruded slightly from her mouth. Jacques' parents watched her worriedly, afraid that she might faint.

"Don't worry," I said. "They all do that."

"Invalids?"

"No," I said. "Artisans."

Lundy's family watched with amazement as her map grew increasingly detailed. When she caught them staring, a subtle smirk appeared on her face, and she began to add some flourishes—a puff of smoke rising from the chimney, and above it, a soaring bird of prey.

When the drawing looked complete to me, I reached down to grab it, but Lundy blocked my forearm with her quill.

"One second," she said, and added one last marking to the page: a vibrant "L," for Lundy.

"I'll bring it to the rebels!" I announced.

"I'll do it," she said, and then, like it was nothing, she walked out of the barn.

The "stolen" map galvanized the rebels, and that night they launched a sneak attack, slipping through the loosened stone and raiding the castle for goods. They escaped sight unseen. And by the time the morning trumpets sounded, and the court became aware of the heist, all that remained of the culprits were a few dusty footprints, and a large shit that one of the men had taken, at great risk to his life, in the middle of a central rug.

The rebels carted the plunder into town, and everyone

ransacked the crates for wine. As the crowd grew drunker, some dressed themselves in stolen outfits and did impersonations of the nobles.

"La-di-da!" said Tall Man. "I'm going to eat food on a *table!*" And everybody laughed as he mimed the way he believed this activity might look.

I spotted Lundy by the wagons. She had found some fresh parchment in a crate and was making sketches of the celebration. Her lips were pursed with concentration, but when she saw me approaching, she broke into a carefree smile.

Her skin wasn't used to the sun, and her cheeks had turned the color of fresh apples. She'd taken off her bonnet, and the sight of her hair startled me, as thick and lustrous as any courtly wig.

"Do you feel bad for betraying the Crown?" she asked me. "After all, they are your kin."

"To tell the truth," I said, "the court can be a lonely place."

"Do you have any siblings?" she asked.

"A younger sister," I said. "But we're not particularly close. She was married to a Swedish king when she was a baby. I sometimes see her face on foreign coins, but that's the extent of our relationship."

"That's sad."

"I'm closer to my father," I said. "Although we

have drifted apart somewhat since he had my mother executed on my seventh birthday."

"Goodness!"

"In his defense," I said, "I don't think he *knew* it was my birthday, and if a minister had told him, he most likely would have postponed her boiling."

"What about friends?"

"I've never had much luck connecting with my noble peers," I admitted. "I think it has something to do with the fact that I'm the prince, and they're required to befriend me by order of the Friend Law. The truth is, until the last few days, I've never really felt like I belonged."

"I feel the same way," Lundy said.

And when she smiled, I could tell she liked me, Friend Law or not.

The oldest of Jacques' boys had found a lyre in a crate and was playing it to the best of his ability, strumming the strings in a crude but pleasing rhythm. His brothers uncovered a pair of silver flutes and played along. They weren't very proficient, obviously. They were just small boys and very, very drunk. But their enthusiasm won over the crowd, and one by one the peasants started dancing.

I smiled at Lundy and offered her my hand.

"Shall we join them?"

"I'm not sure," she said, taking a cautious step back.

"What's wrong?" I asked.

"I don't know," she said, her eyes wide and timid. "It's just that . . . I've never danced before."

"Whoa," I said. "In that case, never mind. We'll be humiliated!"

I withdrew my hand, and we stood there in silence for some time.

But as the music grew louder and more raucous, I felt something loosen inside me, like the stone in the castle wall, and I turned to Lundy and stretched out my hand once again.

"Are you sure?" she said. "Because if you'd like, you could dance with someone else."

I took her hand and looked into her eyes.

"There's no one on earth I'd rather dance with than you, invalid."

I somewhat regretted calling her "invalid," but we both moved past it, and I led her to the center of the crowd. I tried to teach her a basic courtly waltz, but instead she grabbed my hands and started to jump up and down. It felt strange at first, but I followed her lead, hopping around with no pattern. And that's how we danced, making the steps up as we went, sometimes jumping, sometimes spinning, building something strange and new together. And as we twirled and flailed, I looked into her eyes, and in them I could glimpse a brand-new world—a world without rules and constraints, a world without petty social orders, a world governed only by our will. It was a world where we could be whatever we wished, with whomever we wanted, a beautiful world of our own making.

And it was around that time that we heard the royal trumpets.

The heralds were dressed in their usual manner—black boots, green capes, and golden codpieces. We watched with anxiety as they unfurled a lengthy scroll.

The court had become aware of the peasants' theft, as well as the "humiliation of the king's most cherished rug." In order to teach the peasantry to "have more love for their king," the king had decided to sentence them to death. The rest of the speech outlined the various ways in which they intended to perform the executions, a lengthy and horrific list that they recited—somewhat insensitively, I thought—in rhyme. Then, to the peasantry's utter bafflement, they began to speak in Latin. I was a little rusty from my schoolboy days, but I was able to decipher it.

Don't worry, Your Princely Majesty. Just stay where you are. After the army comes and kills all of the peasants, we'll take you back to court. There's a ball tonight, by the way—should be fun.

I smiled weakly and watched as the heralds skipped back to the castle, making use of the Royal Prance—an insulting walk designed to maximize the degree to which the peasants saw their butts.

I turned toward Jacques. He was sitting on the ground, clutching his sons to his chest. Nina tried to calm him, but he shook her away and let out an anguished cry.

"I'm sorry," I said gently. "I was just trying to help."

He grabbed me by the cloak and pulled me so close, I could feel his hot breath on my face.

"You listen to me, you monster," he said. "I hate you. I have always hated you. And as my body boils, I will use my final breaths to curse your name!"

I knew he was having a "bad day," but still, his words stung.

"It's not over!" Lundy shouted, trying to bolster the crowd. "There's got to be some way that we can win!"

There wasn't, of course, but as I glanced at the plunder, it occurred to me that there was still one card left to play. I grabbed a crate of oil paintings and flipped through the canvases until I found one that would do, a portrait of me sitting on a pony. It was a vivid likeness, as detailed as something that Lundy might produce. She ran over to stop me, but it was too late—I had already made up my mind. I held the painting up to the crowd and said, very sadly, "Huzzah."

The peasants gasped as I explained the truth—how I wasn't their kin but a liar and a fraud—a member of the very court that sought to slaughter them.

There was a predictable cry for my death, and

Jacques' death, and the death of his family, and just a whole lot of death in general.

And I said, of course, they could obviously start killing people. But now that they knew my identity, there was a better option: they could ransom me. It was doubtful they would get their original demands. But they could probably leverage my freedom for a general pardon for their crimes.

"We don't want a pardon!" Lundy cried, waving her fist in the air. "We want a fight!"

But everyone else was more in the mood for a pardon. And so Tall Man got on a mule and rode to the castle, and a few hours later, my chariot arrived.

Lundy pleaded with me as I climbed into my jewel-encrusted carriage, urging me to forsake the court and help her build a "better world."

"I will!" I promised. And I explained my new plan—how I was going to change the system "from the inside." I'd take what I learned and radicalize the kingdom until the walls crumbled and we were reunited!

"Your Majesty?" the herald said impatiently.

"Coming," I said.

I wanted to give Lundy a farewell embrace, but there wasn't any time, so I gave a quick bow as I climbed into the carriage. I kept her in my sight as long as possible. Eventually, though, as we galloped up the hill, she grew too small to see. So I turned and watched the castle gates groan open, like a mouth to swallow me whole.

III

The peasants got their pardon, although they had to make several concessions. In addition to releasing me, they had to return the stolen goods, pay for the wine they'd drunk, and also take a formal oath in which they promised to "give up hope in general."

The revolution was over.

Jacques was banished from the castle, and in his place I was given a new valet. My father had decided that none of the local peasants could be trusted, so he selected a servant from my sister's court, named Jens. He didn't speak the language, other than a few phrases they taught him like "Yes," and "I will bring it," and "If I fail to bring it, you are right to kill me."

I was determined to fulfill my oath to Lundy. But I soon began to fall prey to distractions. For example, the night I arrived, the court was celebrating something called a Decadence Ball, which is a contest in which all of the nobles contrive to "out-decadence" one another. Sometimes, while pleasuring ourselves with food and oils, the sensations become so intense that we cover our heads with napkins, out of fear of shaming God. Then we take the napkins off, because what is God going to do to us? We're nobles! And then we dance.

There was a similar ball the next night, and another the night after that, and after a few more months of balls, my father told me it was time to marry. And so a foreign princess was transported to our court, and we were wed in the grandest style. After the ceremony, we introduced ourselves, and she told me that she found me unattractive and had married me entirely for geopolitical purposes. I couldn't help but feel somewhat wounded, but there wasn't much that I could do about it.

Shortly thereafter, my father died of fatness and I succeeded him to the throne. I tried to remember the lessons I had learned in the village, about fairness and so forth, but whenever I attempted to institute reforms, my nobles refused to comply. When I told them that they had no choice, since I was king, they said that I was only king "by virtue of their protection" and unsheathed their swords and stroked them, while staring at me ominously. And they explained that if I tried to take away any of their privileges, they would kill me. And I said, "Yes, I got that from the sword-stroking thing." And they apologized for insulting my intelligence and said that they just wanted to make absolutely sure I was clear about the situation. And after that, we stopped talking about reforms, and I started approving all the new taxes they sent me, without even reading them, including something called the Pain Tax, which sounded like a rough one. And sometimes, late at night, I grew so overwhelmed by guilt, I couldn't sleep, despite all the efforts of my harp men. And I'd toss and turn in bed, clawing at my sheets, thrashing about, like a songbird being boiled in brandy. But gradually, with the help of time and opium, I thought of my wrongdoings less and less.

And the years went by, and I grew so fat, I could barely fit into my throne. And Jens was trying to wedge me in one day when a trumpet sounded in the distance.

Once again the commoners were plotting revolution.

I was handed a pamphlet of their demands, and I flipped through the pages. It was all the usual stuff: freedom, rights, equality, et cetera. I was about to toss the leaflet in the fire when something caught my eye. On the back page, there was an etching of me.

In many ways, the image was generic. It depicted me in the usual manner—eating a baby on the throne while shitting on a flag labeled "The People." But what set the work apart was its accuracy. The likeness was so vivid, it was as if the artist knew me personally. I snapped for a candle to inspect the work further, and that's when I saw it, in the lower right-hand corner, a small but assured "L."

"Bring whoever drew this to me," I commanded. "*Un*boiled."

And so Lundy was captured and brought to me in chains. I was surprised by how much older she looked, although I supposed that I looked different, too, having lost some hair and gained three hundred pounds.

"So," I said. "How's the family?"

"Dead," she said.

"Oh! I'm sorry to hear that."

"No, you're not," she said. "If you cared about your subjects' lives, you wouldn't work them all to death. Their blood is on your hands."

"Fair enough," I said. "Say, I quite enjoyed your drawing of me."

Her expression softened almost imperceptibly.

"It's just a sketch," she said.

"It's better than most," I said.

I asked her some questions and learned about her present circumstances. She had managed to become an artisan, the first of her kind in the village. Mostly she sold images of me, in various baby-eating poses, but she also designed Christmas cards and that sort of thing. I asked her if she'd married, and she told me that she had, and I could tell by the way she said his name that she had found somebody worthy of her charms. And then, even though I feared the answer, I asked her if she ever thought about our time together.

She looked up at me, and for the briefest of moments I thought I glimpsed the old spark in her eyes. But then she shook her head and said, "Not really. It was so long ago, and we were only children." And I knew that there was nothing left to say. Both of us knew that I had failed her.

And so I told Jens to release her, and I watched as she exited the castle. She walked with a cane, and as she jabbed it in the ground, I was reminded of the stick she used to draw with, how she'd etched such lovely shapes into the dirt, where they were doomed to vanish. And it occurred to me that the ways of the world are like the strings of a lyre. No matter how hard you pluck at them, they will always return to their original shape. But in the meantime, there is music.

I decided to hang Lundy's drawing on the wall. Not in a place where people could see it, obviously, since it was pretty unflattering, even by the standards of "King-Eating-a-Baby" etchings. But somewhere private, where I could enjoy it at my leisure. So I ordered Jens to frame it and then meet me in the privy.

And as he hung it up, I sat on the pot and told him my thoughts about the latest revolution—how it was destined to fail, since "the world was the world," and "nothing ever changed." And as I spoke, I noticed that there was something strange about his expression. And I asked him if he felt all right, and he said he was fine, but I could tell he wasn't, and I kept pressing him. And eventually, after several minutes, he admitted, in his broken tongue, that he wished he didn't have to accompany me inside the privy.

And I said, "Huh." Because that had honestly never occurred to me.

And so I said that I was sorry and that, from now on, he didn't have to stand inside the privy. And obviously, he shouldn't stand *too* far from the privy, because I still wanted him to hear my rants, but he no longer had to stand *directly* beside me, as it had been thusly.

"Are you sure?" he asked.

"Yes," I said after some thought. "I am."

And he opened the door and took one small step forward.

CLOBBO

Clobbo peered down at the city lights below. It was a quiet evening in Empire City. But he knew from experience that danger could strike at any turn.

Twenty years ago, on a night as calm as this one, the Space Slugs had invaded and brought the bustling city to its knees. The people had needed a hero—and Clobbo had answered the call. Half man, half ape, with fists the size of boulders, he'd escaped from the laboratory where he'd been created, and charged straight at the enemy, smashing the alien vermin into goo. Within hours, he was standing by the mayor, a key to the city draped around his giant muscled neck.

In the years that followed, Clobbo had rescued the metropolis from multiple alien invaders, including the Space Worms and the Moon Bugs. His rescues grew so frequent that the city built him his own lair, the Fortress of Justice, a towering structure perched on the city's tallest hill.

It had been some time since the last invasion. Clobbo spent most days in silence, patiently scanning the skies. But now, it seemed, the wait was over.

Clobbo could see it flashing through the darkness, the famous Clobbo Signal: a bright neon outline of a giant monkey fist. He let out a roar and jumped through a plate glass window, too eager to wait for any elevator.

At long last, it was Clobbo Time.

Clobbo stood on the steps of City Hall, squinting at the group of officials assembled by his feet. He didn't recognize a single one of them. Eventually, a young woman with glasses stepped forward to introduce herself.

"Hey, Clobbo!" she said, a friendly smile on her face. "It's an honor to finally get a chance to meet you. You're an Empire City legend!"

"Where is Mayor Brock?" Clobbo asked her.

The officials exchanged awkward glances.

"Mayor Brock retired last year," said the young woman. "I'm the new mayor. My name is Susan Chung."

"Oh," Clobbo said. "Clobbo did not know. Clobbo sorry."

"All good!" said the mayor, politely flicking her wrist.

"Where are aliens?" Clobbo asked, craning his giant neck around in confusion.

"I'm sorry for the miscommunication," said the mayor. "There hasn't actually been an alien attack."

Clobbo scratched his hairy brow.

"Clobbo do not understand. You sent Clobbo Signal. That means it Clobbo Time."

"We tried to send you an email," said the mayor. "But it seems like your account was never set up properly?"

Clobbo stared at her blankly.

"Listen," she said, her tone shifting subtly. "There's something we've been meaning to talk to you about."

"Okay."

"Okay. So, you might not be aware, but there's been a pretty serious recession, and we've had to implement a lot of citywide budget cuts."

"Okay."

"Okay. So, unfortunately, part of those cuts is eliminating nonessential costs. And, given the infrequency of alien attacks these past few decades, we just don't think it makes financial sense to continue to operate the Fortress of Justice."

Clobbo slowly blinked his large red eyes.

"But that is Clobbo's lair," he said. "Clobbo need it for defending city."

"It's just too expensive to maintain," she said. "I mean,

it's a sixty-story tower made entirely of glass. It costs a fortune just to clean the windows. Not to mention all the times we've had to replace them."

Clobbo averted his eyes.

"Clobbo sorry Clobbo sometimes jump through windows," he said. "Clobbo from now on can wait for elevator and go down regular."

"We really appreciate your willingness to make that adjustment," said the mayor. "But the decision has already been made."

Clobbo's heart began to race.

"But what happen to Clobbo?" he asked. "Where Clobbo go? *What Clobbo do?*"

"I'm glad you asked," she said brightly. "Because I've got some great news: we're promoting you to management!"

Clobbo eyed her skeptically.

"Management?"

"Yep!"

"Clobbo never manage before," he said, shifting his weight from foot to foot. "Clobbo not sure he know how."

"You're going to do great," she said. "I mean, if you could handle the Space Slugs, you can handle anything!"

Clobbo bowed his head, a bashful smile spreading across his face.

"Really?" he said. "You think Clobbo can handle?"

"Heck, yeah!" the mayor said. "We believe in you. Right, guys?"

Her staff nodded in unison. Clobbo felt his large back straighten.

"What is title?" he asked.

"Great question," said the mayor. "From now on, you are going to be our new...um...what was it, Kevin?" A young aide handed her a clipboard. "Right," she said. "Our new 'Senior Coordinator for the Office of Community Affairs.'"

"Senior Coordinator," Clobbo repeated. "Whoa."

"Yeah, it's a big deal," the mayor said. "And we're giving you your own executive office, on a *very* high floor, and, you know, the whole thing."

Clobbo looked the mayor in the eye, his jaw clenched with purpose. "Clobbo will not let you down," he vowed. "Clobbo will work hard at management. Clobbo will answer the call."

"Clobbo going to need new clothes!" Clobbo said, as he paced across the living room. "Clobbo need tie. Clobbo need shoe."

His wife, Mimi, smiled up at him.

"I'm so proud of you, sweetie," she said. "My husband, the executive."

She reached for his paw, but he was moving too fast for her to grab it.

"Clobbo need to go to bed by ten!" he said. "Clobbo need to leave early in the morning! Clobbo need to allow time for learning new commute!"

"If you're a bit late, I'm sure they'll understand."

"No!" Clobbo roared. "Clobbo cannot be late to first day!"

"You won't be," she said. "I'll make sure of it."

"Maybe you set your alarm, too?" Clobbo asked. "That way we have two alarms: Clobbo's alarm is regular alarm, and your alarm is backup alarm."

"You got it," she said.

"Okay," Clobbo said, relieved. "That is our plan. We will do two alarms."

He took a seat next to her on the sofa, causing his side to droop and her side to rise up in the air. It was their favorite way to sit together, since it put them on eye level. She stroked his furry face while he slowly caught his breath.

"You know," she said, "I was thinking, now that you're in management, it might be a good opportunity to try to strive for a better work-life balance."

"Clobbo do not understand."

"Just, you know, since you've got more power now, maybe you could try to be home sometimes by dinner?

Or even take a Friday off so we can drive to Westchester to see Eli and the kids?"

Clobbo stood up abruptly, sending Mimi sinking to the floor.

"Clobbo cannot take any Friday off!" he said. "Empire City is counting on me!"

He bounded across the carpet.

"Where are you going?" she asked.

"Clobbo go buy *third* alarm clock! Clobbo do not trust our alarm clocks, because they are old! Clobbo go to all-night bodega and buy new alarm clock that is better brand than our alarm clocks!"

"Could you at least take the elevator?" she asked.

But he was already leaping through the window, showering the room with broken glass.

"Clobbo clean up later!" he shouted over the sound of several car alarms.

Mimi stood and watched as her husband swung down the street, leaping wildly from lamppost to lamppost, the metal beams bending under his massive weight. Some teenagers on scooters pointed up at him and laughed. She hoped he was moving too quickly to notice.

Clobbo got to work four hours early. He didn't have a key card yet, so he spent the morning pacing around the lobby, stopping at each mirror to scrutinize his outfit.

He still wasn't fully confident in his executive look. At twelve feet tall and nineteen hundred pounds, shopping for business clothes had been a challenge. Mimi had managed to find him a pair of XXXXL khakis, but when he'd tried them on at dawn, the seams had exploded, leaving him no choice but to tie the garment over his crotch like a diaper. In lieu of a tie, he'd painted a red stripe on his chest. His shoes were buckets.

"Clobbo know he not winning any style points," he'd confided to Mimi. "But hopefully he at least blend in."

After several hours of silent pacing, Clobbo spotted Mayor Chung across the lobby, striding toward the elevator with her usual group of aides. He was so relieved to see someone he recognized, he let out an involuntary roar. The mayor screamed instinctively with fear but quickly recovered her composure.

"Good morning, Clobbo!" she said. "Happy Monday."

"Clobbo ready to manage," Clobbo said. "Clobbo going to manage *everybody*."

"That's what we're counting on," she said cheerfully. "I'll let you get to it."

She nodded at Clobbo expectantly, but he failed to understand this cue for him to leave.

"So?" Clobbo said. "Where we go first? Where is first manage?"

"Well, *I* actually have to get to a staff meeting," she said.

"Okay, great. Clobbo come with. We kill staff together."

The mayor sighed impatiently. "The thing is, Clobbo, you're not really *needed* in the staff meeting."

"Why not?" he asked, some insecurity creeping into his voice.

"Because you have more important things to do!" she said. "And the person who is going to help you do those very important things is . . ." She eyed her row of aides, all of whom avoided her gaze. "Your new assistant . . . *Kevin*."

She pointed at a small young man with acne. He glared at her with undisguised bitterness.

"Do not worry, Kevin," Clobbo said, patting him violently on his bony back. "Clobbo will manage you. Clobbo tell you everything to do for the rest of your whole life."

Kevin stared into the distance as his fellow aides began to chuckle. Clobbo didn't understand the joke, but he joined in anyway.

"Ha ha ha!" Clobbo said. He kept on laughing, long after the aides had walked away, leaving him and Kevin standing there alone.

Kevin led Clobbo to his office on the eighteenth floor. It was smaller than Clobbo had anticipated, and it required some effort for him to squeeze his body through the doorway. But once he saw his desk, his disappointment turned to pride. There, engraved in bronze, was a nameplate with his new official title. *Clobbo the Monkey Man, Senior Coordinator for the Office of Community Affairs.* He rubbed it softly with his giant thumb, trying not to bend the metal.

"I'll give you the Wi-Fi," Kevin said, wearily scribbling it down on a Post-it Note.

"Yes, good," Clobbo said. "Clobbo need that for manage."

"The 'i' in 'City' is a 'one,'" Kevin said. "And the 'a' in 'Hall' is the 'at' symbol."

"Clobbo do not understand," Clobbo said.

"If you want, I could set it up on your laptop," Kevin offered.

"Clobbo do not have laptop," Clobbo said. "Clobbo do not know computers. Clobbo born in lab, and then Clobbo escape from lab and become hero."

"Right," Kevin said. "I know."

"Clobbo escape from lab and then he smash Slugs. They came from space. Clobbo smash them and get key to city."

"Yeah," Kevin said.

Clobbo idly scratched his stomach fur. "Do you want to grab some lunch with Clobbo?"

Kevin raised an eyebrow. "It's ten a.m."

"Clobbo know that!" Clobbo said, waving his giant palm in a show of playfulness. "Clobbo was making joke. Ha ha ha."

"Oh," Kevin said. "Well, listen, I've got a transportation proposal to proofread. But if you need anything, I'll be right outside."

"Okay," Clobbo said.

Clobbo watched as Kevin closed the door, leaving him in almost total darkness. He noticed that the Post-it Note on his desk had been set down at a slightly crooked angle. He attempted to straighten it, but his anxiety made his movements clumsy, and he ended up breaking the entire desk in half. He scanned the room in a panic, looking for a way to cover up the damage. In desperation, he ripped the blinds off the wall and draped them over the crack in the desk. It covered the hole, but now he had no blinds.

"Is everything okay in there?" Kevin called out from the hallway.

"Everything fine!" Clobbo said. He'd meant for the statement to sound casual, but it had come out as violent and deafening. He looked down and saw that his nameplate had fallen by his feet. He tried to put it back where it had been, but his desk was slanted now, like a gabled roof, and no matter where he placed it, the thing just slid right back to the floor.

⋆⋆⋆

"Clobbo have fancy corner office," Clobbo told his wife. "Clobbo have his own nameplate. Everything is good at work and normal."

"That's great, sweetie," Mimi said. She was standing beside him on a ladder, scrubbing the red tie stripe off his chest.

"You will come to City Hall someday," he said. "Clobbo will give you grand tour of new office!" He turned his gaze away from hers and continued in a low voice. "There is problem with desk, where it come from factory with giant crack in middle. It look like somebody smash it, but it come that way. But other than that, everything in the office good."

Mimi held his paw.

"Honey, are you okay?" she asked.

"Clobbo fine," he said. "Why?"

"Because your heart is beating insanely fast," she said. "I can hear it through your chest. It's like literally a thousand beats a minute."

"Clobbo fine," he repeated. "Clobbo have no problems."

Mimi folded her arms and looked him in his pulsing neon eyes. "There's something you're not telling me," she said. "I can tell."

Clobbo hung his head.

"Clobbo stressed out at work," he murmured, finally.

Mimi climbed up a step on the ladder so she could speak to him in a softer tone.

"Sweetie, of course you're stressed," she said. "It's a lot of responsibility."

"Yes," Clobbo said evasively. "That is what it is. There is so much for Clobbo to do. Clobbo have to manage all day. And nobody is good except for Clobbo. So Clobbo have to do everything for everybody, because Clobbo is the only one who knows how to do things."

"Oh, honey," she said. "That sounds really tough. But, hey, I know what'll cheer you up!" She took out her phone and dialed a number. "I finally figured out FaceTime. Eli and Becca are expecting us to call."

"Oh," Clobbo said. "Okay."

He watched as his son and daughter-in-law popped on to her phone.

"Hey, guys!" Eli said. "Thanks for the care package!"

"What care package?" Clobbo asked.

"I sent them something from both of us," Mimi whispered.

"Oh, right, I remember," Clobbo said, smiling into the camera unconvincingly. "You are welcome."

"So?" Mimi said, playfully. "Do you kids have any fun plans for Thursday?"

"What is Thursday?" Clobbo asked.

"It's our anniversary," Eli said tersely. "It's why you sent the care package."

Clobbo groaned into his paws. "Clobbo sorry," he said. "Clobbo distracted with new job. Clobbo manage now."

He expected his son to ask him a follow-up question and was surprised when instead Eli changed the subject.

"So, anyway, Mom, Olivia wants to tell you what *her* favorite part of the package was."

He tilted the phone, revealing Clobbo's granddaughter, a three-year-old girl in a tiara.

"Bubble Wrap!" she said, stomping ineffectively on a sheet of Bubble Wrap.

Mimi clapped her hands and laughed. "You were the same way!" she said to Eli. "No matter what we got you, that was your favorite part!" She nudged Clobbo in the chest. "Remember, honey? How Eli loved Bubble Wrap?"

There was a long pause.

"Clobbo sorry," Clobbo said. "Clobbo was not paying attention. What were you saying to Clobbo?"

Mimi sighed. "I'm sorry," she said to her son. "Your father is obviously a little bit distracted."

"It's cool," Eli said stonily. "I'm used to it. Anyway, it's almost bath time, so we should get going."

"Already?"

"Yeah, Mom, sorry, gotta go."

Mimi shot Clobbo a disappointed look as the phone went black.

"Clobbo sorry," he repeated. But she was already climbing down the ladder, taking the rungs two at a time.

"Clobbo will give you tour of office soon," he called down after her. "Clobbo will show you nameplate. Clobbo will make you proud."

Over the course of the next few weeks, Clobbo began to suspect that his assistant, Kevin, didn't fully respect him as a manager. He never did anything overtly insubordinate. But Clobbo had noticed certain subtle clues, like the way he rolled his eyes whenever Clobbo spoke to him, and sighed, and swore, and whispered, "Unbelievable." Clobbo knew he was probably being paranoid, but he couldn't help but feel insecure.

Clobbo tried his best to win Kevin's respect, frequently visiting his desk to try to manage him.

"Clobbo need numbers," he would say. "You give Clobbo numbers now."

"Which numbers?" Kevin would respond.

"You tell me," Clobbo would say. "You are supposed to know which numbers. You find out which numbers and you show to Clobbo!"

"I don't know what you want," Kevin would say. "I have no idea what you're talking about."

"Okay," Clobbo would say.

These conversations left Clobbo feeling rattled. When he got home from work, he always made sure to ask Mimi how her day had gone. But the moment she started to respond, Clobbo found himself replaying his latest talk with Kevin in his head, ruminating over every little detail. Had he said something that gave him some cause to be embarrassed? He wished there was some way to tell.

One morning Clobbo ran out of red paint and had to paint his tie on using ketchup. By the time he finished swinging to work, it was almost 10:15. He was relieved to find his floor was empty; there was no one there to see his late arrival. But his calm was shaken by a distant peal of laughter. He followed the noise, and found himself walking down a hallway he had never seen before. At the end of it was a large conference room, crammed with at least fifty of his colleagues. Mayor Chung was sitting at the head of a long table, with Kevin by her side. Her mood was chipper, but when she saw Clobbo, her expression grew noticeably tense.

"Oh, hey, Clobbo!" she said, waving awkwardly. "Happy Monday."

"What is this meeting?" Clobbo said. "Nobody told Clobbo there was meeting."

"Huh," said the mayor. "Well, that's probably just because it's not for your department."

"It seems like it is Clobbo's department," he said. He pointed over her shoulder. Behind her, projected onto a large screen, was a PowerPoint slide, reading, "Office of Community Affairs."

"Clobbo is Community Affairs," he reminded her. "And this is Community Affairs."

"Huh," the mayor said, nervously drumming the table with her fingers. "That's so odd. It must have been an oversight by... Kevin."

She smiled apologetically at Kevin, but he refused to make eye contact with her.

"I put it on his iCalendar last month," he said, staring straight ahead. "It's not my fault if he didn't check it."

Clobbo wasn't sure what an iCalendar was, but he could feel everyone's eyes on him.

"It was not on Clobbo's iCalendar!" he said defensively. "Kevin did not tell me, because he is bad assistant!"

"Okay," said the mayor. "We can sidebar this—"

"No!" Clobbo said, doubling down. "It cannot wait, because it is important! Kevin, you are always making mistake! You never give Clobbo numbers!"

Kevin folded his arms and cocked his head.

"What numbers would you like, Clobbo? Tell me, and I'll happily provide them."

"I want numbers for Community Affairs!" he shouted.

"Literally every piece of data is available on the

server," Kevin said. "If you bothered to read the daily briefings—"

"Clobbo reads daily briefings!" Clobbo shouted. "Clobbo reads it more than *you,* Kevin, because you are bad at job!"

"Okay," Kevin said. "If you read the daily briefings, then what did you think of this morning's Banana Report?"

"Clobbo hate Banana Report!" he said.

"Yeah, well, there was no Banana Report," Kevin said.

Clobbo's stomach lurched as a ripple of involuntary giggling spread across the room. Most people managed to stifle their chuckles, or modulate them into coughs. But the initial burst of laughter continued to echo in Clobbo's head. He could feel sweat pouring down his back and pooling in his giant khaki diaper.

His fists instinctively began to flash and pulse, and for a moment he considered smashing everyone to death. But his anger quickly passed, replaced by a dull and throbbing nausea. He blinked his big red eyes, trying to hold back his tears.

"I'm sorry, Clobbo," said the mayor. "It's my fault. I should have made sure you knew about this meeting."

"It is fine," Clobbo said. "Clobbo is the one who should be sorry." His voice began to crack. "Clobbo should have read daily briefings. Clobbo should have read Kevin's Banana Report."

Kevin hung his head, his anger toward Clobbo finally giving way to full-on pity.

"Clobbo resign," Clobbo said.

"You don't have to do that!" the mayor said. "You're still a big part of the team!"

"Please," Clobbo begged. "Stop lying to Clobbo. Stop torturing Clobbo. Let Clobbo go while he still has some dignity."

Clobbo headed for the door, but his angle of entry was off, and he got stuck. The mayor watched with guilt as he struggled to force his body through the doorway, clumps of plaster falling all around him. Eventually he let out a sigh.

"Clobbo need five people to push on his butt," he said quietly. "Two on left side, two on right side, and whoever strongest go in middle."

The mayor and Kevin stood up, along with some other aides, and worked to shove Clobbo through the door. It took several minutes and the application of a tube of hand lotion, but eventually Clobbo was dislodged. There was a cartoonish popping noise as he fell forward, landing on his hands and knees. As he crawled away, his khaki diaper caught on the edge of a desk, leaving him completely naked. He didn't have the space to turn around, so all he could do was keep on trudging down the path, whichever way it led.

★ ★ ★

Clobbo spent the next two months in bed.

Whenever Mimi asked him about his decision to "retire," he gave her cryptic answers.

"Clobbo decide he need new challenge," he would say. Or, "Clobbo need space to start new chapter."

Mimi tried to feign enthusiasm, but she knew that he had failed. And worse, on some level Clobbo knew she knew.

One day, a package arrived from City Hall. Mayor Chung had sent Clobbo a "Farewell Key to the City." Mimi tried to get Clobbo excited about it, but he saw the gift for the pitying gesture that it was. He shoved the box in the corner of their bedroom and left it there, unopened.

He hadn't felt so low since he was a kid and being subjected to torture experiments by the evil scientist who made him. It had not been a happy childhood. It wasn't anything specific Dr. Skull had done, but on some level, he'd just never felt completely valued. It wasn't until he started fighting aliens that he developed anything resembling self-esteem.

He remembered how proud he'd been the first time he saw his face on the cover of the *Empire Enquirer*. They were the ones who'd dubbed him Clobbo. He'd never had a nickname before. When he was growing up, everyone had always just addressed him by his birth name, Monkey Torture Test Subject 12X. At first, he wasn't sure he liked being called Clobbo. But the more he saw it printed in the headlines, the more he fell in love with it. He even began to speak in the third person, saying "Clobbo" at the beginning of basically every single sentence. It was a way of reminding himself that he had an identity. That in spite of where he'd come from, he'd somehow found a purpose in this world.

It wasn't lost on him that the box from City Hall had been addressed to "Klobo." The intern who'd mailed him the key was probably too young to have ever seen his name in print. The next generation would most likely never hear it uttered. The Clobbo name was gradually being erased, like a Space Slug being pummeled into goo.

It was while these grim thoughts were swirling through his brain that his wife's phone rang abrasively. Clobbo forced a smile as his son and granddaughter popped onto the screen.

"Thanks for the birthday present," Eli said.

"What birthday present?" Clobbo said. "Clobbo did not send present."

Mimi sighed. "I sent Olivia a doll from both of us."

"Oh," Clobbo said. "Clobbo sorry."

"Anyway," Eli said. "I can't talk for long. Olivia is having a T-A-N-T-R-U-M."

Clobbo watched as the toddler screamed, her nostrils flared, her small fists clenched. He felt a similar way.

Mimi smiled into the camera. "Maybe I can cheer her up?" she said. "'Old MacDonald had a farm, ee-i-ee-i-o...'"

Clobbo wandered away from the couch, his wife's strained singing fading in the background. He couldn't handle talking to his family right now. What was the point? He had nothing to offer to them or to anybody else. He was climbing into bed when he tripped over his package from the city. He idly tore it open and turned the key over in his paw. It was the cheapest model he had ever seen; aluminum, probably, or maybe even plastic.

"Thanks for the memories!" read a note from Mayor Chung, typed on generic Empire City letterhead. She hadn't even bothered to sign it with a pen. He crumpled it up and threw it in the trash. He was about to crawl under the covers when he caught sight of something else inside the box. He stared at it, the wheels slowly turning in his mind. Tentatively, his palms began to pulse.

"'And on that farm he had some chicks...'"

He could hear Mimi losing steam in the living room, her singing drowned out by the toddler's swelling cries.

"Oh, well," she was saying. "We can try again some other time..."

"Do not hang up!" Clobbo shouted.

He hurried back out into the living room, clutching the cardboard package in his hands.

"What's going on?" Eli asked.

"Oh, your father got a new Key to the City," Mimi said. "Guess he wants to show it to you."

"No, that is not it," Clobbo said. "Look, little girl. Clobbo have something for you."

He reached into the box and took out a large plastic sheet. The girl's sniffling started to subside. "Baboo has Bubble Wrap!" she said.

"Who is Baboo?" Clobbo asked, craning his giant neck around.

"That's what she's been calling you," Eli explained. "I don't know why."

The toddler pointed her finger at the screen.

"Can Baboo do Bubble Wrap?" she asked.

Mimi nudged her husband indulgently. "That shouldn't be a problem!" she said. "You might not know this, but your grandfather used to pop squishy things for a living—"

Baboo raised a paw, gently waving off the praise. He looked into the phone and nodded at his granddaughter.

"Baboo can do Bubble Wrap," he said. "And Baboo will do it now."

The toddler watched as her grandfather laid the sheet over his knee and rolled his fist over the plastic, setting off a long cascade of pops. His granddaughter sighed contentedly, and he smiled at her with pride.

"More?" she asked.

His smile faded.

"Baboo is not sure if there is more," he said. "That might be all there is."

The girl's lower lip began to quiver.

"Baboo will see if there is more!" he said frantically.

Eli and Mimi watched as he rummaged through the box, tossing aside the flimsy key and digging through the Styrofoam peanuts. When he got to the bottom, he was so relieved that tears came to his eyes.

"There is more," he said, roughly wiping a paw across his face. "Baboo has more. Baboo can do more."

Mimi rubbed her husband's furry back as he took out the Bubble Wrap and carefully set it on his knee.

"Baboo will do more," he vowed to his granddaughter. "You watch Baboo."

He took a deep breath and held up a fist for the camera.

"Baboo do more now," he said. "Now it Baboo time."

CASE STUDY

London, 1886

It is rare for a physician to encounter a specimen whose condition reduces him to tears. But some cases are so horrific that even a hardened Man of Science cannot help but feel his emotions stirred. What follows is a true account of the most appalling case ever observed by this physician, a case so rare and tragic that it haunts him to this day.

The subject was first observed at a common Soho sideshow. He had spent his youth under the control of a cruel mustachioed showman, who had forced him to live inside a cage and display himself for profit. It was as if nature had conspired to riddle the poor creature with as many abnormalities as possible. His cranium was swollen to twice its natural size, and the features of his face were contorted into a grotesque grimace. His forehead was bulbous, his jawline crude and jagged. The subject's given name was Joseph Merrick, but society had cursed him with a different appellation: the Elephant Man.

It was determined by this physician that the subject deserved a better life. And so the poor creature was rescued from the showman and transported to the Royal London Hospital so that he might find a new beginning.

The subject confessed to this physician that his greatest pain was, in fact, not physical but emotional. A lifetime of solitude had robbed him of the social kinship most men take for granted. And so it was determined by this physician that a visitor should be brought to see the subject, and thus bring improvement to his state of mind. This visitor would have to be someone of high noble character, gifted with patience, grace, and tact. To that end, it was determined by this physician that his own wife, Anne, ought to be enlisted.

After being warned of the subject's vile condition, Anne was led into his hospital room. It is a testament to her poise and charm that she did not scream or recoil. Instead, she engaged the subject in happy pleasantries and even consented to shake his hand, ungloved. It was observed that her presence seemed to elevate the subject's mood. Within moments of her arrival, the subject even managed a small smile, an expression this physician previously thought him to be physically incapable of forming.

It was observed by this physician that the subject's hand gestures grew increasingly animated as he interacted with his wife. It was further observed that he made prolonged eye contact with her. It was generally observed by this physician that the subject seemed confident talking to his wife.

As the minutes passed, it was observed by this physician that some of the subject's questions to his wife were pretty personal. For example, at one point, the subject asked her about her sister and then spoke about his own sister in a manner that implied that they were going through similar situations with their sisters. It was observed by this physician that his wife seemed impressed by the subject's opinions about her sister. It was additionally observed that she laughed at all his jokes about her sister, even though she did not like it when this physician made jokes about her sister. It was noted that she seemed to find the subject's jokes hilarious.

After observing much laughter by his wife, this physician ventured a joke of his own, to the effect that maybe his wife should get going, given that it was "visiting *hour,* not visiting *day.*" It was observed by this physician that his wife did not laugh at this joke, although it was objectively superior to the jokes that had been made by the subject, and that, evidently, his wife's bar for comedy was lower for the subject than it was for this physician.

As the physician's wife exited the hospital room, she noticed a crude model of St. Philip's Church that the subject had built out of coarse strips of paper. The physician's wife praised the model, and the subject described it as an example of how "sometimes, that which is ugly can grow to appear beautiful." It was observed by this physician that his wife seemed impressed by the subject's comment, even though it was obviously a line. It was further observed that the subject's model of the church was not particularly good and was basically like something a child would do for school, and it wasn't like the subject was some great artist, he had just glued together a few strips of paper, and he had probably only done it so he could say his line about how ugly things were beautiful, and it was observed by this physician that in general the subject kind of sucked.

That night at home, it was observed by this physician that his wife brought up the subject all the time and seemed to be obsessed with him. When this fact was noted by this physician, his wife confirmed she thought the subject was "impressive." When pressed for evidence of this notion, the physician's wife pointed to the "adversity" he had overcome. It was noted by this physician that many people overcome adversity. For example, some people work hard to become physicians, which requires one to go to medical school, a task considerably more challenging than sitting around in a sideshow all day, getting free food just to hang out. It was suggested by the physician's wife that she return to the hospital tomorrow, to visit the subject again. It was stated by this physician that he was too busy to arrange said visit. At this point, the physician's wife announced she intended to visit the subject anyway, alone. It was observed by this physician that she seemed more excited for this visit than she had been for anything in years, and that he hadn't seen her smile so brightly since the very first moments of their courtship, when they'd met at a garden party and he'd asked her to go promenading.

It was observed by this physician that his wife seemed distracted all night. It was observed that she drank more than her usual one glass of wine. It was observed that she retired from the table early. It was observed that she went to bed without saying good night.

★ ★ ★

The next morning, it was observed by this physician that his wife came to visiting hours wearing a new dress. It was observed that the subject had left his door open and was conspicuously reading a thick book of poetry. It was observed that, when she greeted him, he pretended at first not to notice her, as if he were so engrossed in his cool poetry book that he could not even hear words. It was observed by this physician that his wife seemed impressed by this ruse and totally bought it.

It was observed by this physician that his wife presented the subject with expensive art supplies, and that he in turn presented her with a drawing he had made of Lord Byron, a poet she had mentioned during her previous visit. When she professed amazement at his "great memory," the subject made a joke to the effect that "an elephant never forgets." It was observed that she laughed so hard at this joke that everyone in the whole hospital could hear her, including the physician's colleagues, who avoided eye contact with the physician, probably because they were embarrassed on his behalf because his wife was laughing so hard at another man's joke that it was basically like she was having sex with him in front of everybody.

It was observed by this physician that visiting hours

were over, and so he gave an order to the nurses to go from room to room, enforcing protocol. Shortly thereafter, the physician's wife walked up to him and expressed disappointment that she had to stop talking to the subject in the middle of "a great conversation." It was noted by this physician that it was weird that she wanted to keep hanging out with the subject. At this point, she laughed and said, "Oh, my God. Don't tell me you're *jealous*."

Her statement was refuted by this physician, but at the same time he did note that it was odd how much time she was spending with this guy she had just met.

"This is crazy," she said. "You really think I'm *attracted* to him?"

It was noted by this physician that it certainly appeared that way, given her actions and behavior.

"He's the most deformed person in history," she said. "Besides, he's clearly gay."

It was noted by this physician that his wife had no hard evidence that the subject was gay.

"He wears a cape," she said.

It was noted by this physician that (a) the subject most likely wore the cape to cover his deformities and (b) capes no longer carried the same connotations they once did. There were lots of straight guys who wore capes, and he had read an article about it. Additionally, it was noted by this physician that the subject had been observed checking out her ass.

"That's just the way his skull droops," she said. "His cranium is tilted downward."

It was noted by this physician that he had never observed the subject check out male asses and that it was only her ass that seemed to make his cranium "tilt downward."

"So you watch him all day long?" she asked. "And check to see which asses he looks at?"

The question was posed by this physician as to whether she had ever once heard the subject say explicitly that he was gay, or mention a boyfriend, or anything like that.

"He's not going to come out and say it," she said. "It's Victorian England. He's got enough going on."

It was noted by this physician that the subject seemed like a pretty open guy and that if he were gay, he would probably be up-front about that fact, given that he was up-front about everything else, like his opinions on poetry and art and whatever the fuck else he said to try to impress her during visiting hours.

"So I can't have any male friends," she said. "That's what you're saying. I have to live my life in total solitude because of your paranoia."

It was noted by this physician that she could be

friends with whomever she wanted, but that she and the subject appeared to be becoming *more* than friends, and as evidence of this fact, he pointed out that she was wearing lipstick, which was something he'd never once observed her doing.

"I wear lipstick all the time," she said. "You just never notice."

Over the next few weeks, it was observed by the physician that his wife had started sleeping in the downstairs bedroom. Meanwhile, she continued to visit the subject daily at visiting hours, frequently wearing new outfits, all of which, objectively, were designed to showcase her ass. It was further observed by this physician that she had lost at least ten pounds and gotten into basically the best shape of her life.

It was additionally observed by this physician that his wife had increased her correspondences, and was writing and receiving messages constantly, and that even though she claimed she was writing all the letters to her sister, it was obvious that the letters addressed to his wife were written by somebody with a deformed hand. It was also around this time that this physician started drinking ether and cocaine.

During an intense binge of narcotics, it was determined by this physician that the subject should return to the sideshow so that his interactions with his wife might cease. To this end, he walked down to Soho and explained the situation to the showman, who listened in silence while silently twirling his mustache.

"It might be an emotional affair," he said.

It was stated by this physician that he was unfamiliar with the term.

"It's where they're not having sex, but it still counts as a betrayal. Also, sometimes, it *leads* to sex. Like the emotional intimacy is a prelude to physical consummation."

The question was posed to the showman as to whether or not he thought that the subject was gay.

"No way," he said. "I mean, I guess he might be bi? Like, you know, he's into art and poems and stuff. But he's definitely had girlfriends. He was actually with this one girl who was insanely hot."

The physician drank a bottle of cocaine.

"Whoa," the showman said.

It was suggested by this physician that the subject return to the sideshow.

"Not a chance," the showman said. "The last thing I need is a guy like that around, trying to steal everybody's girlfriend. How did he even meet your wife in the first place? Isn't he confined to a hospital bed?"

It was admitted by this physician that he had been the one to introduce them.

"Fuck me," said the showman. "What were you thinking?"

It was noted by this physician that he deeply regretted it and had no idea what he was going to do, and that he was completely freaking out, and he couldn't believe that they were doing him like this.

"You've got to put your foot down," said the showman. "You're her husband; tell her she can't hang out with him anymore. And tell him the same thing. Tell him to back the fuck off."

It was noted by this physician that if this ultimatum were issued, it could have the effect of driving them further into each other's arms.

The showman shrugged. "At this point, honestly, what have you got to lose?"

The decision was made by this physician to confront his wife and the subject at the next visiting hours. When he climbed the stairs to the subject's room, he observed that the door was closed and all the blinds were drawn. When the door was kicked open by this physician, it was observed that his wife was sitting beside the subject on his bed, a poetry book spread out over their laps.

A statement was made by this physician to the effect

that he was sorry to interrupt, and they could go back to fucking each other in a minute, but first they should know that he wasn't a fool, and also, he couldn't believe that they would both do him like this. At this point, the wife of the physician began to apologize to the subject for the physician's behavior. It was noted by this physician that she was the one who should be apologizing for trying to fuck the Elephant Man, and he reiterated again that he couldn't believe she was doing him like this. At this point, the shouting began to grow intense, and the physician and his wife grew increasingly loud, until they were finally interrupted by the subject, who said, "Dr. Treves, this is crazy. There is nothing going on between us. Anne and I are just friends, and it's totally platonic. Anne, tell him."

It was observed by this physician that his wife seemed disappointed to hear the subject characterize their relationship in this manner.

"Yeah," she said bitterly. "Of course. Who would ever be in love with me, right?" It was observed by this physician that, despite her caustic tone, her eyes were damp with tears. It was further observed that the subject was growing frustrated.

"Okay, look," he said. "I'm not really sure what's going on, but you guys obviously need to have a serious conversation to figure out what's happening with your marriage. Because I feel like I'm just getting sucked into something here that has nothing to do with me, and that's not fair. And I can't go outside, because I'll be attacked by a mob, but I'm going to wrap my cape around my face so you guys can talk this out in private."

And when he put on his cape, it occurred to this physician that it was the first time in weeks he had talked to his wife one-on-one. And it was further observed that, although they'd been married for years, they seemed almost like strangers to each other. And to break the ice, the physician offered his wife some of his ether, and she drank some right out of the bottle, in a quantity that suggested that her tolerance had gotten really high, and that, like the physician, she had lately been consuming lots of ether. And after a long, fearful pause, the question was put to her by this physician as to whether or not she loved the subject.

"I don't know," she admitted. "But I thought that he loved me. And maybe it was wrong to seek that attention. But it was all I had."

And she noted to this physician that he had been neglecting her for years, and in many ways taking her for granted. And it was observed by this physician that she had a point, and that perhaps he had been too focused as of late on his career, and his case studies, and his perpetual hunt for specimens unique enough to write about. And it was noted by this physician that his priorities had become displaced.

And it was observed by each of them that, in some ways, they had both been at fault, and that although their marriage was in crisis, that did not mean that it could not be saved. And they related these developments to the subject, and he nodded and said that he had heard the entire conversation because his cape was not particularly thick.

And it was observed by this physician that the root of their problem had been one of mutual insecurity. They both had assumed that there was something wrong with them that made them undeserving of their partner's love. And it was observed by this physician that perhaps at times everyone felt this way: like an unloved outcast. And when he said this, the subject rolled his eyes a bit, and the physician kind of backtracked and admitted that there were maybe degrees to which people felt like outcasts. But the point was that both the physician and his wife had felt lonely for some time.

And so they agreed to go to couples therapy, and they began to try new exercises, like doing a mandatory date night once a week where they had to take turns asking each other questions that they did not know the answer to. And it was kind of weird at first, but over time, it was observed by both of them that it was also kind of fun. And gradually, their marriage began to regain strength, like a patient recovering during a lengthy convalescence. And one night, at some Italian place, she made a joke, and the physician laughed so hard that people looked over from the other tables, and she began laughing as well, which made them both laugh more, and he observed that she looked just as beautiful as the day they'd met, when he'd first noticed her at that garden party, a specimen so lovely it felt as if all of nature had conspired to create her, a creature so unique it could stir the emotions of even the most hardened Man of Science, a remarkable rarity, amazing to observe, incredible to see.

RAISED BY WOLVES

In 2003, a group of hunters discovered a young woman in Siberia who apparently had been raised by wolves. Scientists were unable to explain the child's origins, but an examination indicated that she was approximately eighteen years of age and in surprisingly good health given her unusual upbringing. Researchers named the woman "Lauren" and worked with authorities to assimilate her into human society.

With effort, Lauren managed to catch up to her peers, both socially and intellectually. She was able to obtain a college degree. By the age of thirty-five, she had married an insurance actuary named Gabe and given birth to a healthy daughter. Lauren never again interacted with the wolves that raised her, except when they came over for Thanksgiving.

* * *

Lauren was considering whether or not to take a Klonopin when her husband shuffled in, straining under the weight of a dead elk.

"You didn't have to get that," Lauren said.

"It's the least I can do!" Gabe said in a chipper Boy Scout voice. "It's so cool of them to come all the way out here."

He dumped the carcass on the coffee table, shattering several bowls of nuts and olives. Lauren sighed.

"What's wrong?" Gabe asked.

"I just don't understand why we always have to accommodate their needs."

Gabe shot her a scolding look. "Because they're your parents. And they're our guests."

Lauren popped the Klonopin and washed it down with a swig of Pinot Grigio.

"Look, I get it," Gabe said. "Parents are hard. Mine drive me crazy, too. I mean, my dad, with those puns? It's awful."

"I think my parents are worse," Lauren said. "I mean, growing up with them was a full-on nightmare."

"Maybe it's just gotten worse in your memory?"

"It was documented by scientists," she said, some frustration creeping into her voice. "There've been multiple books about it and an award-winning documentary."

Gabe massaged her shoulders in a way that managed to somehow make her feel even more tense.

"I know your folks aren't perfect," he said. "But they came all the way from Siberia. They've been running and swimming for months, and they'll be gone in half an hour. The least we can do is be civil, right?"

"I guess," she said.

"Great!" he said, sealing the agreement with a condescending forehead kiss. "Besides, it might be fun. I mean, you've got to admit, your dad's stories are pretty epic."

Lauren smiled tightly as Gabe whirled around the living room, setting out the napkins and the tarps. She'd told him all about her screwed-up childhood. The barking, the growling, the total lack of structure and support. Her parents had never been abusive, but it had still been a dysfunctional home. Her therapist had confirmed it.

"They did not see you," she said. "And you were not heard."

Still, while Gabe was aware of her parents' transgressions, he had never actually witnessed any. Her parents had both mellowed considerably with age. Her father had stopped howling at the moon following his stroke, and after a few false starts, her mother had finally quit drinking. Lauren knew she should be grateful for their progress, but somehow it galled her. By rehabilitating themselves, they had robbed her of an audience for her suffering. It was one more deprivation—the latest in a chain stretching all the way back to her childhood.

Two piercing canine howls sounded in the distance.

"I think that might be them," Gabe said. "Do you want to get the door?"

"You can get it," she said.

She refilled her wineglass to the brim. She could hear her parents laughing with Gabe in the foyer, making the usual small talk about travel. She wanted to delay the encounter for as long as possible, but her parents quickly sniffed her out and loped into the living room.

"Sorry we're late!" her mother said. "You know your daddy—he didn't want to ask for directions!"

"It's a good thing I had my better half!" he said.

Lauren cringed as her parents nuzzled. Growing up, her father had cheated on her mother constantly, with her friends, her neighbors, and once with a log that had a hole in it. And now everyone was supposed to pretend like their marriage was perfect?

"So, how's everything?" her father asked her. "How's work?"

"It's fine," Lauren said.

There was a two-second pause, and Gabe rushed to fill it.

"Work's better than *fine,*" he said, smacking Lauren's arm with an annoying amount of force. "Honey, tell them your big news!"

"It's nothing," Lauren said.

"It's not nothing," Gabe protested. He turned to her parents and gestured at her like a game show host. "You are looking at Verizon's newest Regional Marketing Communications Manager!"

Lauren's parents tackled her and licked her face.

"We're so proud of you!"

"Thanks," Lauren said.

"So, what does this mean?" her father asked. "You get to hunt bigger animals?"

"I'm not a hunter," she said. "I work for Verizon. It's a telecommunications company."

"Ah, gotcha," he said, lowering his eyes. "I'm sorry I got it wrong."

"You're not wrong," Gabe told him reassuringly. "She got a twenty percent raise, which is sort of like the human equivalent of hunting bigger animals. Right, honey?"

"I mean, I guess," Lauren said noncommittally.

"Well, that's great!" said her mother. "I'm not surprised. We used to always say, 'There goes Lauren—our little genius!' "

"Huh," Lauren said.

Gabe shot her a warning look, which she ignored.

"What?" her mother asked.

"Nothing," Lauren said.

"It's okay," her mother said. "You can say it."

"I just don't remember you ever saying that," she said. "My memory, in fact, is that you never named me."

Her parents hung their heads.

"Would anybody like to eat this dead elk's ass?" Gabe asked.

"Thanks," her father said. "I'm not really hungry."

"Okay, I'm sorry," Lauren said, rolling her eyes. "I shouldn't have said anything. I should have remembered the family rule: Never say anything about anything uncomfortable, ever."

Lauren's father put his tail between his legs. "Maybe coming here was a mistake," he murmured. "Maybe we should just jump out the window."

Lauren shrugged. "Wouldn't be the first time that you left."

"Sweetheart," he said pleadingly. "We went over this in therapy. The reason I left the family had nothing to do with you. It was a period in my life when I was confused. I thought that log with a hole in it *was* your mother. I literally thought the wood was her body and the moss on it was her fur. It was a crazy time in my life. I had rabies."

"So *I'm* supposed to feel sorry for *you* now?" Lauren asked. Despite the wine and Klonopin, her hands were shaking.

"We're not asking for sympathy," her mother said. "And if there's something you need to say to us, we're here to listen. Right, darling?"

"Yes," her father said. "We are prepared to honor your emotions."

Lauren clenched her fists; she hated it when they used therapy jargon.

"Let's start with my leaving," said her father. "Tell me why it makes you so upset."

"Oh, I don't know," Lauren said sarcastically. "Maybe because it happened on my fucking birthday?"

Her parents eyed each other subtly.

"Let me guess," Lauren said. "You don't remember."

"Honestly, no," her father said.

"So you're saying that I made it up?"

"I'm not saying that!" he said, raising his paws defensively. "It totally could have happened the way that you remember it. I'm just saying *my* memory is different."

"Okay, fine," she said. "What's your memory of the day you left?"

"Okay, well—and again, this could be inaccurate. We're talking about something that happened a long time ago, and my brain is the size of a pine cone, and I have no understanding of time or numbers. But *my* memory of that day is, I was walking through the woods. And then the big yellow god that lives in the sky shined hot. And then there was a smell, like, 'Okay, time to go.' And so I ran into the wet place that is cold. And again, that might not be a perfectly accurate description of what happened. But that's what I remember."

"That's what I remember, too," her mother said.

"There's no point in doing this," Lauren said. "Every time, it just leads to frustration."

"We're frustrated, too!" her father said. He sighed. "I'm sorry for growling just now. I was flooded."

"That's all right," Lauren muttered. "Go ahead."

"Thank you," he said. "My point is: I know we weren't great parents. We were young, and we were wolves, and we didn't always know what we were doing. But every time we see you, all we do is apologize, over and over, and it's not easy. In order to do it, we both had to learn to talk English, and it hurts our throats and sounds insane. Just hearing my voice right now coming out of my mouth—it's incredibly unnatural and disturbing. So if you want us to keep saying sorry, with these weird, choking animal voices, we will. Because we *are* sorry. But at a certain point... the ball is in your court."

The room fell silent, allowing them to hear a distant squeak.

"Sounds like someone's up!" Gabe said, grateful for an excuse to flee the living room. He ducked out and returned a moment later, holding their three-year-old daughter, Haley. She was gripping a small orange ball—the source of the squeaking. Her eyes were bleary from sleep, but when she saw her grandparents, she let out a squeal and buried her face in their fur.

Lauren was surprised that Haley even remembered who they were. She'd barely spent any time with them. There was the Thanksgiving before this one, and that Memorial Day when they'd flown her to Siberia because Gabe's sister was getting married, and there were no kids at the wedding, and it was just the easiest childcare option. Lauren had expected Haley to be homesick that weekend in the tundra, but somehow she'd managed to enjoy herself. It didn't hurt that her grandparents had spoiled her rotten. Lauren had asked them to limit Haley's screen time, but they let her watch as many cartoons as she wanted. They claimed it was because they didn't understand what screens were and had no way of differentiating between an iPad and any other reflective surface, like a puddle or an eye. Lauren suspected they were lying, but somehow she found herself charmed by their indulgence of her daughter. In their coddling of Haley, she sensed a desire to make up for the past, a subconscious awareness that there were wrongs that needed righting.

Haley tossed her orange ball across the room, and her grandparents obediently fetched it. It was surreal to Lauren to see her folks so docile, but of course to her daughter it made perfect sense. She didn't see her grandparents as the vicious wolves they were. To her, they were just Papa and Gam Gam.

Someday she'd have to tell Haley the truth about her childhood, and the trauma she'd endured.

Or maybe she wouldn't. Maybe she'd tell a different narrative, one that focused on the things that they'd got right. How they'd fed her, sheltered her, and defended her from hawks. For all their dysfunction, she'd ended up turning out okay. In some ways, her parents' flaws had even contributed to her success. (She knew, for example, that her essay about them was a major factor in her getting into Brown.)

Haley was about to throw the ball again, when instead she walked over to her mother.

"Now Mommy throw," she said, pressing the soggy ball into her hand.

Lauren turned it over in her palm. It was hard to tell if the drool was her parents' or her daughter's. Haley had some new teeth coming in. Lauren had recently brought her to the dentist and the X-ray of her child's jaw had shocked her. There wasn't anything out of the ordinary, but it was disturbing to see all those adult teeth embedded in her skull, a lifetime of canines and molars, waiting their turn to erupt. It would be years before the teeth broke through her gums, decades in some cases, with braces, retainers and extractions along the way. Why couldn't humans come out fully formed, with everything they needed? Why did it have to take so long and hurt so much to finish growing up?

She gazed at her parents, now crouching low on the carpet in a show of deference. In wolf years, they were four hundred years old. She wondered what their upbringings had been like. They'd been raised by wolves, too, of course. They'd never spoken about their parents, and it occurred to Lauren only now that she had never asked.

She held up the ball and her parents stared at it with tired yellow eyes. Their panting was labored, but their pupils were focused, tracking the ball as she tentatively traced it through the air. She could hear them faintly whimpering, as plaintive as two pups begging for scraps.

"Throw, Mommy," Haley pleaded. "Throw."

Lauren lifted the ball high, feeling its heavy, sticky weight. Then she took a deep breath and let it go.

SCREWBALL

The best thing about playing baseball is the chow. They give you three bucks a day for meal money, and you get to pick the things you eat. For breakfast, I had flapjacks with butter, biscuits with gravy, beefsteak with eggs, six rolls with butter, two sides of liverwurst, oatmeal, ketchup, and plenty of potatoes. I never go hungry like before.

It feels funny being so far from the orphanage. The good news is, I'm not the only rookie. There's another new player, named Jack, and they have us rooming together. Even though we're both nineteen, I really look up to him. He's got what they call "discipline." Every day he wakes up at four a.m. and does two hours of German squats. Then he drinks raw eggs and runs up and down the staircase till he pukes. He is a serious teetotaler: no drinking, smoking, chew, or even sweets. He does have a girl named Bella that he writes to at Miss Parker's Finishing School in Buffalo, but he says their relationship is "noble" and "above suspicion." If anyone's gonna make the team, it's him.

I was in knots our first practice. I've only ever played orphan ball, and there's guys here who played up in the majors, like Deek Derrick from Philly and Speedy Ball from the Cleveland Naps. I wanted to ask them all sorts of questions, like did they ever meet Cy Young, but Jack warned me not to speak to any vets. You have to "earn their respect" first. You'll know you've been accepted, he told me, when they give you a nickname. I asked him if he had a nickname yet, and he said, "Sort of." And I asked, "What does that mean?" And he said that some of the fellas called him Junior. And I asked him why, and his voice got kind of quiet, and he said it was because his daddy was the manager.

And I said really loud, "Why didn't you tell me your daddy was the *manager*?" And Deek and Speedy looked over at us. And I asked them if *they* knew that Jack's daddy was the manager, and Deek nodded slowly and said, "Yes, we're all aware."

I tried my best to copy Jack all day so that I wouldn't screw up. But I ended up embarrassing myself anyway. I was taking batting practice with the other pitchers, and we were all supposed to bunt. But when I got up to the plate, I saw all those vets staring at me, and I got so nervous I forgot to lay one down, and I just swung the bat like regular, and the ball went all the way over the fence, and the rail tracks, and some houses, and ended up splashing in a river. And everyone got really quiet, like the nuns at the orphanage used to when I screwed up doing my sums. And Mr. Dunn stared at me and said, "My God." So I said I was sorry, and that I'd remember to bunt next time, and I started to run to get the ball, because, you know, that's Orioles property. But before I got past the infield, Deek whistled for me to come back. And he patted me on the shoulder and said, "Don't worry about the ball. We got plenty of 'em, babe."

And I turned to Junior and gave him a thumbs-up, because now I had a nickname, too, just like him!

And since then, that's what everyone's been calling me. Babe, or the Babe, or Babe Ruth.

1, Caporal; 2, Ball; 3, Russell; 4, Twombly; 5, Jarman; 6, Lidgate; 7, Derrick; 8, Cottrell; 9, McKinley; 10, Egan; 11, Capron; 12, Danforth; 13, Cree; 14, Daniels; 15, Davidson; 16, J. Dunn, Mgr.; 17, Pedone; 18, Gleichmann; 19, Parent; 20, J. Dunn, Jr.; 21, Ruth; 22, Kelly, Mascot.

BALTIMORE TEAM—INTERNATIONAL LEAGUE.

1914 Baltimore Orioles, AA International League, Spring Training

Babe Ruth, #21, P, OF

Career Major League Batting Average: .342

Total Major League Home Runs: 714

World Champions: 7

Jack Dunn, #16, Manager

Career Minor League Coaching Wins: 2,107

Jack Dunn Jr., #20, LF

Career Minor League Batting Average: .175

That night, I saw Junior writing numbers in a book. I asked him about it, and he said he likes to track his daily progress using "mathematics." And he flipped through the pages, and it had all his records from his high school, and he showed me how he'd worked to make sure his batting average went up every year, so by the time he was a senior, he was hitting almost .250. And he asked me what I'd batted for St. Mary's, and I explained that things weren't really like that at the orphanage. I just hit and pitched when people told me to. And then one day, I was splitting lumber in the work yard, and Brother Mathias came by with Mr. Dunn and said, "George, throw the ball for this nice man." And he handed me a baseball, and I threw it over a building, and then I found out I was going to get to ride a train.

We were about to go to sleep, when a clump of dirt smacked against the window. So I jumped out of bed and looked outside, and all the veterans were there! And they said they were going to a tavern. And I said I wasn't sure if Junior went for taverns but that I would ask him, and they said, "Don't ask Junior. We don't want him to come. Don't invite him, just come without him, please. Don't bring him." And I turned to Junior, who was sitting right there, and told him how swell I thought it was that the veterans supported him so much in his decision to be a teetotaler. And he sighed and said, "Thanks, Babe."

I was nervous to go out with the veterans, but it turns out Junior was wrong about them. They were the most welcoming group I'd ever seen. They kept slapping me on the back and offering me whiskeys. I wanted a drink, to stop my heart from pounding, but I figured I'd lay off the stuff, to follow Junior's example. So I drank Coca-Cola and listened while the guys told me stories about their playing days. And I asked if they had ever met Cy Young. And they said they hadn't, but Mr. Dunn "sure had" and when I asked what they meant, they said that Mr. Dunn once shut him out 2–zip!

I had no idea Mr. Dunn had been a ballplayer, but it turns out he pitched a few years in the majors, and he would have been an all-time great, but one day his elbow burst into fifty pieces. He tried to keep pitching after that, but he couldn't throw curveballs anymore, they just didn't have the same bite, and also batters could tell when he was about to do one, because he would scream really loud, you know, from agony.

When he started in the majors, his nickname was Peppy Dunn, because he was always pacing around the dugout, clapping his hands, with a big smile on his face. But after his injury, people started calling him Screaming Dunn, and then Pain Dunn or Sad Dunn, and now he didn't have a nickname anymore, he was just Mr. Dunn, the manager of the minor league Baltimore Orioles.

I asked the guys why Mr. Dunn didn't try to manage in the majors, and they said no front office would give him a shot on account of his record in the minors. The Orioles have been losing for years in Double A, and last season they finished almost twenty games out, even behind the Rochester Hustlers, which is really saying something, because their team is like a carnival team, and they've got a clown at second base, with the red nose and the shoes and the whole deal, and everyone agrees his act is pretty good with all the handkerchiefs, but you don't want to lose to a guy like that at baseball. Mr. Dunn's only chance of getting noticed by the majors would be if we won the whole league, by a lot.

"Maybe we will," I said. "We got some good guys, right?"

"It doesn't matter," Deek said. "You're only as good as your weakest link."

And I got nervous and said, "Are you guys talking about me?" And for some reason, everybody laughed.

Junior was still awake when I got home, writing letters to Bella at Miss Parker's Finishing School in Buffalo. And I realized, with cuts coming soon, that it might be our last night together. So I said to him that I sure hoped I made the team, but if I didn't, I'd write him from the orphanage, care of the Baltimore Orioles, and he could send me letters from the road, with all his box scores, so I could follow along when he was making good. And at least, when I was old and gray, I'd be able to tell everyone I'd met a baseball legend, the great Jack Dunn Jr.

The next day was the last day of tryouts and Mr. Dunn made an announcement. He said he'd heard a rumor that some players were concerned that he was "biased." But it wasn't true.

"The Baltimore Orioles are a meritocracy," he said. "Everyone gets the same shot. It doesn't matter if you're a veteran, a rookie, or, you know... whatever."

A few guys turned toward Junior, and he looked down at his cleats.

"In order to guarantee fairness," Mr. Dunn went on, "I have developed a series of drills that are mathematically designed to test each player's aptitude." Then he blew his whistle, and it was time to go to work.

I tried my best at his drills, but I'd never done them before, and it was hard to keep everything straight. For example, one time we were doing throws from deep center, and I was supposed to toss it to the cutoff man at second, but I forgot and just threw it past him on a line drive straight into the catcher's mitt, and the catcher fell backward from the force. And someone stood and said, "Our game is forever changed. Nothing will ever be the same." And everyone kind of bowed their heads in silence for a while, like the nuns used to at St. Mary's when the priest talked about Jesus. And I was, like, "What's happening?" Another mistake I made is that I hit a ball too hard and it exploded.

The toughest drill was grounders. Mr. Dunn's getting on, but he can still hit with pop and he was laying down all kinds of junk at us. The rollers were fine, but the one-hoppers gave everyone fits. Even Deek and Speedy missed a couple. I handled mine all right, although there was one that hit a pebble, and bounced real high over my shoulder, so instead of fielding it with my glove, I had to jump up and barehand it, then throw it around my body in a single twirling motion.

Junior was up next. I could tell he was nervous, but he handled the rollers like a pro. It was pretty impressive to watch. It was almost like he could tell in advance which side his dad was gonna hit to. I wondered if they'd ever done the drill before.

When they were finished, Mr. Dunn said, "Perfect score! Unbelievable!"

Junior smiled and was about to leave the infield when Deek said, "What about one-hoppers?"

Mr. Dunn's eyes got real round, like a frightened rabbit's. But then he smiled wide and said, "Thank you so much for reminding me, Deek. I almost forgot about the one-hoppers." Then he turned to Junior and said, a little softly, "You ready, kiddo?"

And Junior cleared his throat and said, "Yes, sir."

And Mr. Dunn took out a bucket of balls.

"These are one-hoppers now," he said.

"Yes, sir," Junior said again. And he pounded his mitt, to show that he was ready. And Mr. Dunn hit over a one-hopper and it bounced right by his son.

Deek and Speedy both started to snicker, and Junior's face turned red, but Mr. Dunn didn't seem to notice any of that. He just smiled at Junior and said, "It's all right, here comes another!" And he hit over the next ball, but that one got through, too.

And Mr. Dunn smiled even wider and said, "Great effort!" And he kept shouting out things like that after every miss, like "Good hustle!" or "Way to stay with it!" or "Nice technique!" but by the middle of the bucket, he'd run out of things to say, so he just started saying, "Nice try," over and over.

"Nice try . . . nice try . . . nice try . . ."

Mr. Dunn hit the last ball right at Junior, but it bounced off a pebble and started to sail past his shoulder. Junior tried to barehand it, like how I had done, and he was really close to pulling it off, but at the very last second, instead of snagging the ball, he fell down hard on his face, and his pants and jock split open, and his butt popped out, and everyone kind of gasped, because there was his butt. And he just kind of lay there on the dirt for a while, with his face in the mud and everybody staring at his naked butt.

And there was a long pause, and then Mr. Dunn blew his whistle and said tryouts were over.

Deek said Mr. Dunn always nailed the roster to the tree behind the backstop so everyone would know where to find it. It could be ten minutes or it could be ten hours, depending on how long it took Mr. Dunn to make his picks.

I decided to stand by the tree and wait there as long as it took. After a few minutes, though, I started to get pretty hungry, and then I thought, *If they're sending me back to the orphanage tomorrow morning, I better spend all my meal money* now, *in case they try to take it from me.* So I went to the hotel restaurant and gave the maître d' all the coins I had and told him to bring me as much food as it could buy me, and it didn't have to make any sense, it could be all mixed together, in a bucket or whatever, and I didn't care if I got the shits. And then I ate four steaks with cream sauce and three bowls of pudding and fish of the day and turtle soup and shrimp and tapioca. And in the end, I still had four cents change, so I went to a grocer to spend it up on candy. But as I was reaching for the licorice, I saw a big display of eggs. And I thought about Junior, and how he loved to drink eggs in the morning, for his puking exercise, and I decided to get him some eggs as a present. And I stuck them in my pocket, and it was around that time I heard a hammering noise.

When I saw the lineup nailed to the tree, I got so nervous, I felt like drinking a whole gallon of whiskey. But then I thought to myself, *Well, if I don't make the team, at least I got to ride on a train and see a big city like Fayetteville and go on an elevator and try tapioca, so I should be thankful.* Then I said a prayer to God and read the list and there I was:

George Herman Ruth, Pitcher/Outfield

And I kept reading my name, over and over again, to make sure I wasn't reading it wrong. But I wasn't—that was really my name, written all fancy in type, just like in a newspaper. And I was so relieved, I felt like crying. And all I could think was: I can't wait to show Junior.

So I ripped the roster off the tree and ran up to our room. He was oiling his glove in the dark, and when I told him the news, he nodded solemnly and said, "Congratulations, Babe. You deserve it."

And I said, "Thanks!"

And then there was a long pause, and he said, "What about me? Did I make the team?"

And I said, "Of course!"

And he pumped his fist.

And I said, "I mean, I haven't checked the roster yet. But I figure."

And he sighed and said, "Would you please check the roster?"

So I said, "All right." And I smoothed out the roster and scanned through all the names. And I couldn't find him anywhere. But then, at the bottom, I saw his name scrawled down in pencil.

"Yep, here you are!" I said. "Jack Dunn Junior."

"Oh, thank God," he said. And he closed his eyes and slid against the wall, all the way down to the floor. "I take it I didn't get shortstop," he said, chuckling.

"Deek's playing short," I said.

"Figures. Am I in left?"

"No."

"Center?"

"No."

"Right?"

"No."

"Then what am I?"

"It says here you're the ice boy."

And I pointed out his name on the bottom of the list:

Jack Dunn Jr.—Ice Boy

I wanted to ask him what an ice boy was, but I was too embarrassed, since I figured it was probably some professional term that I should know about, especially now that I was a real baseball man. But whatever it meant, I could tell Junior was excited, because he kept shaking his head and saying, "Oh, my God."

And I smiled at him and said, "I know! We're living our dreams!"

And I gave him a bear hug, and there were all these loud crunches, and when I saw our gooey clothes I broke out laughing, because I'd forgotten all about the eggs!

It turns out "ice boy" means pretty much what it sounds like, just a boy who carries around ice for the team. It isn't a very baseball-heavy job, but Mr. Dunn said that's the whole point. It's important for Junior to "stay fresh" so we can have "some talent in reserve" in case of injury. So far no one's gotten hurt, although I think Deek might be getting sore, because at least four times a game he calls out, "Ice boy!" and snaps his fingers until Junior brings him a slab.

I'm really glad that Junior made the roster, because I'd be lost without him. The guy is a baseball expert, and I am always asking his advice on stuff I need to know, like how do you autograph a baseball, or talk to reporters, or pose for a painting, or wave to a crowd at a parade.

This morning they wrote about me in the paper, and I had no idea what it meant, so I said, "Hey, Junior, what does it mean when they write that my 'rags-to-riches story is in some way the story of America itself'? Is it good, or is it bad?"

And he said, "It's good, Babe."

And I said, "Phew!"

We started the season 5–0, and all the credit goes to Mr. Dunn. He is always coming up with good strategies. Like when I was pitching against the Jersey City Skeeters, he told me to "strike everyone out," and that ended up working really well for us.

We kept on winning that whole month, against the Montreal Royals and the Providence Grays, and it got to where other teams were running scared. In Rochester, the Hustlers were so nervous, the clown didn't do his handkerchief routine, he just wore a mitt and played regular. We beat them 12–2, and when we got back to the hotel, there was a telegram for Mr. Dunn from one of his old friends in the majors, congratulating him on the streak. He didn't say anything, but he got this huge grin on his face, and he started to pace around the lobby, clapping his hands, and Deek said, "Hey, look, it's Peppy Dunn."

The next morning, he called a meeting and said we gotta focus—no booze and no late nights—because we're tied for first with the Buffalo Bisons, and we were gonna play them soon. Junior doesn't smile much during meetings, he mainly just stares down at his ice, but when Mr. Dunn said "Buffalo," he looked up and beamed in a way I hadn't ever seen before.

And as soon as we got back to our room, he made a telephone call to Miss Parker's Finishing School, and when Bella came on, he told her he was coming to her town. And he asked her if she'd gotten all his love poems, and if she remembered their night together at the mixer, and how they'd danced the turkey trot with the moon up overhead, and did she think about him often the way that he thought about her? And then she said something back, and Junior's smile kind of faded, and he held out the receiver and said, in a whisper, "She wants to talk to you, Babe."

So I said hello, and it turned out that she had seen my picture in the paper, and we talked for a spell about baseball, and what I liked better, throwing strikeouts or hitting home runs, and she asked me about my body, and how I got my muscles how they were, and if I was that strong in real life or only in the pictures, and, long story short, Bella said she would visit our hotel when we got to Buffalo!

So I hung up and told Junior the good news, how he was going to get to see his girl. And he clenched his jaw and said, "She's not my girl." And I was pretty surprised, because I thought he liked her a whole lot. But he said, no, he never really did, they just danced once at a mixer, and it was only a turkey trot, and he'd just been writing her to be polite, because really he thought she was nothing special, and he didn't have any feelings for her at all. So I said, "Well, in that case, is it okay if I take her out? Because she seems nice." And he closed his eyes and whispered, "I don't care what you do. I don't care about anything anymore." So I said, "Great!"

I was excited to go meet this Bella. But as we rode to Buffalo, I started to get nervous, because the truth is, I'd never been out with a lady, especially not a fancy one who'd finished at a school. And I started to worry about things, like what kind of place should I take her, and what if I run out of meal money, and what if I say the wrong thing, or laugh at the wrong time, and what if she doesn't like me? And by the time we pulled into the station, I was so scared, I almost ordered a whiskey. But things turned out to be a lot easier than I thought. Bella was waiting in the lobby of the hotel, so that made things simple, and when she saw me, she said I didn't have to take her out and instead we should "get straight to screwing," because her curfew was at nine and she wanted to "go hard." So I turned to Junior, who was standing right there, and asked him if he minded sleeping on the couch, and he said it was fine because "life has no meaning," so I said, "Great."

So then me and Bella went up to the room and went at it, and I don't know what they teach at finishing school, but she definitely knew more than I did about a lot of things. And it was fun, but after a couple of hours, I said, "I can't take this anymore," because even though I'm a professional athlete, I was starting to get really sore. And she said, "Don't stop, Babe," and I said, "I gotta, I'm really hurt down there." And she said, "Well, maybe you can ice it, like a muscle." And I said, "Where am I going to get ice?" But then as I said that, I realized, hey, this is a pretty lucky coincidence, because I happen to be buddies with the best damn ice boy in the minor leagues!

So I put on a towel for modesty and opened the door, and there was Junior on the couch, reading the Bible, with earmuffs on and the radio going full blast, and I asked him to please carve me some ice (and I explained why I needed it, how I was sore from all the screwing, with Bella). And he said, "All right." And he reached under his bed and pulled out his ice chest and carved me out a piece. Then he carved out a second piece, and put it in a glass and filled it up from a large bottle of whiskey. And I said, "Aren't you a teetotaler?" And he said, "I am nothing." And he drank the entire glass in one swallow.

And that's when I clocked that maybe there was something going on with Junior, like maybe there was something causing him some kind of trouble.

So I went back to my room and explained to Bella that I had to go spend some time with Junior, but that I would write her letters from the road, and she said not to bother with the letters, but next time I came to Buffalo, she was going to bring her friend and come for longer and do more things. And I said, "All right." Then I went to check in on my friend.

I found him lying on the floor, next to his half-empty bottle of whiskey. He had his glove out, and he was staring at it, just turning it over in his hands, like he was looking for something that was lost. And he asked me, "How do you do it? Is there a secret?"

And I said, "Yes. You gotta put your mind on something else. When she's going, you just picture yourself like on a trolley, and that way you can last."

And he closed his eyes and said, "I meant baseball."

And I said, "Oh. Well, yes, I've got one trick to playing, but I don't like to tell it."

And he grabbed me by the shirt, with both of his hands, and he pulled my face so close, I could smell the whiskey on his breath, and I was surprised at his strength, because he's just a little guy, and he shouted at me, "Please, you gotta tell me, please!"

And when I looked into his eyes, I could see by the tears that he was desperate. So I said, "Okay, but if I tell you, you gotta swear that you won't tell anybody." And he promised me he wouldn't tell a soul. So I checked the hallway, to make sure no one was listening, and then I closed the blinds, too, just to be safe, and I told him my big secret to baseball:

"Whenever I'm pitching, or hitting, I always make sure to put a little mustard on it."

And then I leaned back and smiled, like, "You're welcome."

And he took a long, slow breath and said, "That does not help me."

And I said, "Why not? Just do it like I said. Put mustard."

And he stood up and shouted, "I don't have any mustard, you idiot! Not everyone has mustard! Some of us are born without mustard!"

And I didn't understand why he was so angry, because up until this moment, everything between us had been perfect. So I said, "Please don't be mad at me, Junior. You're my best friend."

And he said we weren't friends, we were enemies. Then he climbed into bed and pulled the covers over his head and turned off the lights.

And it felt like my first night at the orphanage,

after my folks sent me away for being "incorrigible." I didn't know any of the other boys, and when I cried, they screamed at me to "shut it," because they didn't like me yet, since it was before they had seen me play baseball.

I try not to think about that time, but sitting there with Junior, it came back in a rush, and I felt so lonesome, my heart began to pound, like the engine of a train, faster and faster—*thump-a-thump-a-thump-a-thump*—and it got so bad, I did something I knew I shouldn't do.

I reached for the whiskey.

When I woke up, I knew something was wrong, because instead of being in my bed, I was underneath a bridge. There was a nice bum there, and he explained that I had shown up with the bottle empty, naked, and said, "I have no friends, and this is where I live now."

So I asked the bum how to get back to the baseball team. But he didn't know anything about that. So I thought, *Well, I'll find Junior. He'll know what to do!* But then I remembered that he didn't like me anymore. And for the first time in a while, I was on my own.

So I ran back to the hotel, and the bellhop said, "Babe, you need to put on clothes, and also, the team left without you." So I ran to the station and jumped on the train while it was moving. And I was relieved that I had made it, but after a few hours, I noticed that the conductor was talking funny, saying things like "bonjour-this" and "bonjour-that." And by the end of the day, I realized that maybe this train didn't go to Baltimore. So I jumped off the train and ran up to a woman in a field and said, "Help me, I'm Babe Ruth, the baseball player," and she was like, "bonjour-this" and "bonjour-that," and I thought, you know, this isn't great. And the snow was coming down, so I ran into a barn and I figured, well, I guess I'm gonna die.

But then a farmer came and told me, "This is Canada," and he gave me overalls and put me on a train, and after a couple more days, I got back to a place where people knew baseball, and some kids recognized me from the paper, and they took me to Oriole Park.

There was almost no one in the stands, and the people inside looked sour. I could see from the scoreboard that we'd dropped to third place, and we'd lost the last five straight, and we were about to lose another, since we were down 9–0 in the bottom of the ninth with two outs and nobody on base. Mr. Dunn was sitting in the dugout, with his head in his hands, not looking peppy at all. And I felt pretty rotten until I saw a sight that cheered me up: Junior was coming up to bat! And even though he'd said that we were enemies, I couldn't help but root for him.

The umpire called him to the plate, and he ran to the batter's box full speed, like he was stealing home. Then he stuck his pinkie in the air, adjusted his stance, and nodded to show that he was ready. He missed on the first pitch, and the second one, too. But the third pitch, he managed to graze with the top of his bat. The ball rolled slowly down the first base line, and the catcher and pitcher stared at each other, hoping the other one would pick it up. But neither of them did, and Junior ended up with an infield single! And everyone cursed and rolled their eyes, including people in the Orioles dugout, because I guess they wanted the game to be over. But Junior didn't seem to notice. He was standing on the bag, smiling big and bright. It was only when he heard me cheering that his smile went away.

After Deek popped out to end the game, I made my way down to the field. I was afraid Mr. Dunn might be mad at me for missing so many games, but when he saw me, he didn't yell or curse, he just threw his arms around my neck and started kissing me on the face, sort of like I was a baby. And he asked me if I could play tomorrow, and I said, sure, and then he started dancing, just shaking his hips back and forth and singing, "Ha-cha-cha, ha-cha-cha," and kind of spinning around in a circle and making little guns with his fingers. Then he called out for Junior.

And Junior ran over, and I smiled at him, but he wouldn't even look at me. And Mr. Dunn told him that going forward, he was going to need to take "more responsibility" on the team. And Junior grinned and said, absolutely, and he'd already scouted the next three pitching staffs, and he couldn't wait to take them on. And there was a long pause. And Mr. Dunn explained that Junior misunderstood, and that what he meant by "more responsibility" was that he wanted Junior to stop playing baseball and instead watch me 24–7, and follow me around, and take care of me, sort of like my "nursemaid."

And Junior said, "Sir, with all due respect, I disagree with this baseball decision." And Mr. Dunn tried to cut him off, but Junior kept talking, about how he was making good progress, and the more Mr. Dunn tried to interrupt him, the wilder Junior got, and he took out his notebook, and flipped through all the pages, with all of his statistics, and some graphs and charts he'd made about his "escalating rate of improvement," and Mr. Dunn said it all looked swell, and that he was very proud of him, but that he needed Junior's help to win the league, and Junior said, "If you want me to help you win, you can put me in the lineup!" and Mr. Dunn got kind of flustered and said, "That's not where you belong."

And I thought Junior would get angry, but instead he gave a weird smile and said, "Yeah, all right. I'll watch the Babe."

And I threw up my hands and cheered, you know, because I was happy me and Junior were best friends again.

I wanted to go back to the room to rest, but Junior said we should "celebrate our new arrangement." So I followed him down the street to downtown Baltimore. And I asked him where we were going, and he said it was a special surprise. And then he led me through a door, and it was full of people, and when they saw me they all shouted, "Babe!" And Junior explained that it was a special bar, for Orioles fanatics. And while he was talking, someone came up to Junior and asked him how he could get a replica Baltimore Orioles uniform like he had, since it looked just like the real thing. And I said, "That's not a replica, Junior's on the team." And everybody laughed really hard. And then Junior said, "Hey, who wants to buy the great Babe Ruth a drink?" And pretty quick, the bartender came over with a whiskey and said it was on the house. And I said to Junior, "Are you sure this is a good idea? Because the last time I drank whiskey, I ended up naked, in a foreign barn." And he said, "Babe, don't you trust me?" And I said, "Of course I trust you. Why wouldn't I?" And so I drank the whiskey, then another, and another, and before I knew it, I'd lost track of Junior, and I looked around the bar all night, but I couldn't find him anywhere. And whenever someone tapped me on the shoulder, I turned around fast, hoping it was him, but it was always a fan and never my friend.

When I woke up the next morning, I was relieved because at least I could see Baltimore out the window. But as my eyes focused, I realized there were iron bars in front of it and I thought, you know, that isn't great. And it turned out that I was in jail, for doing crimes.

I could see Mr. Dunn through the bars, talking to a cop. His hands were clasped like he was praying.

"Are you *sure* it was the Babe?" he asked.

"I'm afraid so," the cop said. "We have hundreds of witnesses all over town, and they all said the maniac was wearing an Orioles uniform."

"But he's not wearing one," Mr. Dunn said.

And the cop explained that I wasn't naked when they found me, that just kind of "happened somehow" during the "madness of the chase."

And Mr. Dunn put his head in his hands and groaned, and I've never heard anyone ever sound so tired. And I asked him if it was too late to make it to the game that day. And he reached through the bars and patted me on the shoulder and told me I wouldn't get to play games anymore. The league had a "morality clause," and the commissioner was going to kick me out for breaking it. And I asked if I could still hang around and help the team practice, or maybe be the ice boy. And he said he didn't think that was a good idea, and it would probably be safest for me and the citizens of Baltimore if I just went back to St. Mary's. And I started to cry, because that was the thing I was most afraid he'd say.

And then the door swung open, and it was Junior, and he was dressed to play, and he said they better go, or else they'd miss the game. And Mr. Dunn said, "What happened? How did you lose him?" And Jack shrugged and said, "I tried my best, but he's incorrigible." And Mr. Dunn wandered off into the hallway in a kind of daze. And Junior was about to follow him, but I reached through the bars and grabbed his wrist, because I realized it was my very last chance to say goodbye.

And I said I was sorry about last night, I didn't mean to get lost. And he said, "It's fine, Babe," and he tried to walk away, but I held on tight because I had some more to say. And I told him how happy I was that we had met, and that if anyone deserved to make it to the big leagues, it was him, and that I would follow his career the best I could, even though we didn't get newspapers at the orphanage, other than the scraps they put out for wiping in the shitter.

And he swallowed and said, "Thanks, Babe."

And then I said, "There's one more thing." And I looked around the jail, to make sure no one was listening, and then I fessed up that I had one other secret to baseball, and it was an even better secret than the "mustard" one, and I'd never told it to anyone before, but since my career was over, he could have it. And he leaned in close, and I whispered the secret through the bars, and this is what the secret was:

"You don't always want to hit everything with mustard."

And then I smiled and leaned back, like, "You're welcome."

But I could tell he was confused like before. So I kept going.

"It's like this," I said. "When they give you an easy fastball, sure, you always want to hit the thing with mustard. But when they give you a nasty screwball, the way that spins, you'll never hit it over the fence, no matter how much mustard you give it."

"So, what do you do?" Junior asked.

"You lay off the mustard," I said. "And you shift your body, and you tap it over to the other side. See, that's the big secret to baseball! Don't swing at the pitch you wanted. Swing at the pitch you got."

And I wasn't sure if Junior liked the secret, because

he was silent for a while and kind of looking off into the distance.

And then the cop came back with Mr. Dunn, and they said it was time to write up my confession. And I said I was happy to, but they would have to help me because I didn't remember doing anything.

And then Jack took a step forward, and he had a look in his eyes I'd never seen before, kind of like a hitter when he knows he's got the pitcher's number. And he said, "That's because you *didn't* do anything, Babe." And he turned to the cop and said, "*I* did."

And he said that the cops had the wrong guy, and that the Orioles uniform everyone saw belonged to him! And Mr. Dunn whispered to him, "Son, you don't have to do this." And Junior ignored him and took out a pen and said he was willing to sign any confession. And the cop shrugged and said, "All right, but we need to go through the counts, one by one, and put them all in the public record." And Junior said, "Go right ahead."

"Public intoxication?"

"That was me."

"Public nudity?"

"Me."

"Public urination?"

Junior hesitated. By this point, some newspaper people had come over so that they could photograph his face.

"Public urination?" the cop asked again.

"Yes," Junior said softly. "That was me."

"Shitting in a mailbox while shouting out, 'Special delivery.'"

"Yes," he said. "Me."

And the cop added up all of the fines and said that the Dunns owed sixty dollars. And then Junior turned to me and smiled. And I said, "Why are you smiling? You have a serious drinking problem. Last night should be a wake-up call for you to get help." And then Junior laughed, and I did, too, because I was just so happy we were friends again.

And the cop let me out of my cell, and Junior checked his watch and said, "We better hurry, Babe's pitching in an hour." And I thought Mr. Dunn might be mad at his son for all his crimes, but instead he threw his arms around him and tousled his hair and slapped him on the back, like he'd just hit one out of the park.

Junior got kicked out of the league, but even though he couldn't play anymore, Mr. Dunn kept him in the clubhouse. And Junior started using his mathematics book to help the rest of us play better, like figuring out when in the order we should bat, and which pitchers we should steal on, and when to shift the infield, and we started winning games by even more runs than before. And Junior got so busy that one time Deek shouted out, "Ice boy!" and Mr. Dunn said, "Not now," because, you know, his son had more important things to do.

And we got back into first place, and one day, after beating the Bisons, three guys in suits walked up to the dugout, and they said that they were from the Red Sox, and they wanted to have a chat with Mr. Dunn.

And Junior turned to his dad and said, "Congratulations." And Mr. Dunn said, "I couldn't have done it without you, kiddo." And he turned to the Red Sox men and said he couldn't wait to bring his "first-place spirit to the major leagues."

And the main Red Sox guy said, "There's been a misunderstanding. We aren't here to hire you. We're here to sign Babe Ruth."

And Mr. Dunn pleaded with them that he deserved a shot, because he had coached his team into first place, by a lot. And they said they didn't "doubt his coaching abilities," but in their view, the Orioles' success had less to do with coaching than with the fact that they had found a "once-in-a-lifetime baseball freak."

And Mr. Dunn started talking really fast, like a chicken auctioneer, and he said he didn't have to be the manager, he could be a pitching coach, or a first-base coach, and the Red Sox guys sighed and looked at each other and shrugged, and eventually one of them smiled tightly and said, "How about this? You give us Babe Ruth, and you can come up to Boston and be sort of like an 'honorary coach.' You can sit in the dugout and wear a cap, and the whole thing. And, hey, your boy looks like a ballplayer! Maybe he can come up to Boston, too? And we'll give him a tryout, and a uniform, and you can both say you're major leaguers!"

And Junior said, "Dad, I've got an idea." And he told me to wait with the Red Sox men while they talked in the next room.

And when the Dunns were gone, I turned to the three guys and asked them straightaway if they'd ever met Cy Young. And they said they had! And then I asked them if they'd ever met Ty Cobb. And they said they had! And then I asked them if they'd ever met Walter Johnson. And they sighed and said, yes, they had met all the famous baseball players. So I asked if they had ever met Homerun Baker. And we talked like that for a few more hours and it was a really fun afternoon.

When the Dunns came back, Mr. Dunn said that they could sign me to the Red Sox, and they didn't have to let him coach or give Junior a tryout.

And the Red Sox men looked confused and said, "Well, what do you want, then?"

And Mr. Dunn said, "Twenty thousand dollars."

And the Red Sox men got angry and said, "What the hell do you need that kind of money for?"

And Mr. Dunn nodded at his son and said, "Jack, you tell them."

And Junior flipped through his notebook and listed all the stuff they were fixing to buy, like a new dugout, and better uniforms, and "modern training equipment," and an "automatic ice machine," and everything else they would need to turn the Baltimore Orioles into a winning ball club. And the Red Sox men could tell that the Dunns weren't about to back down, so they wrote them a check, and that's when I found out I was going to get to ride another train. And it was going to be first-class this time, which meant all the food I wanted, even if it cost more than three dollars. But I was pretty nervous, because I'd never been to a big city like Boston before, and I didn't want to go there by myself. So I asked the Dunns if they could come with me, at least for a little while. But they said they couldn't, because that's not where they belonged.

And I started to get worried, because what if the Red Sox were making a mistake by signing me? And what if I screwed up and let everyone down? And Mr. Dunn told me not to worry, because the Red Sox didn't go around signing just anybody. But I was barely listening by then, and my hands started shaking, like when my daddy left me at St. Mary's and I realized he wasn't coming back. And I was just about ready to lose it when Junior put his hand on my shoulder and said, "Don't worry, Babe. They're going to love you in Boston."

And I said, "How do you know?"

And he looked me in the eye and said, "Because you're Babe Ruth. And you're the greatest player in the world."

And all of a sudden I wasn't afraid to ride the train. So I gave the Dunns a hug and told them both to write to me, care of the Boston Red Sox. And I turned to the baseball men and said, "I guess I'm ready."

And now it's five years later and everything is different. I only play baseball in big stadiums, and when I leave the field, the crowds all come and follow me around. And it is a pretty swell life, like, for example, sometimes they'll put up a billboard of me, or put me in a picture show, or build a statue of me out of bronze. But no matter how much fun I'm having, I never forget about my friends, the Dunns, and whenever I think of it, I write them a letter, care of the Baltimore Orioles. And last month, they wrote me back and sent me a picture of them holding up a trophy. And they said that they missed me in the lineup, but it seems like they're doing all right, like they figured it out, like they found a way to win.

1921 Champion Baltimore Orioles

119 Wins

47 Losses

1st Place, AA International League

Jack Dunn, Manager

Jack Dunn Jr., Co-Manager

EVERYDAY PARENTING TIPS

We've all been there. The teeth are brushed, the pj's are on, and the blankie is *juuuust* right. You're tiptoeing out of the nursery when suddenly you hear, "Mommy, Mommy, there's a monster under my bed!" You let out a sigh. Looks like that new episode of *The Bachelorette* is going to have to wait. :(

Children have always been afraid of monsters. But lucky for you, our experts are up to the challenge. So let's open up that mailbag!

Is it normal for my child to be afraid of monsters?
Yes. If anything, it's evidence of a healthy imagination.

How do I convince my child there's no such thing as monsters?

Just be patient. By the age of five, your child should understand that the monsters she's afraid of are not real.

What if the monsters she's afraid of *are* real?
Unfortunately, this is becoming increasingly common in the aftermath of the Great Monster Uprising that took place earlier this year. Ever since the creatures descended from the Dark Place, their presence on Earth has become an unavoidable aspect of our daily lives. If your child is afraid of an actual, real-life monster, such as Gorgog the Annihilator, or Ctharga the Eater of Souls, try to explain to her that, although those monsters are obviously real, the likelihood of them attacking her is only moderate.

Should I restrict my child's media access to keep her away from upsetting imagery?
Most parents agree it's wise to shield kids from scary content. At the same time, experts warn it may be futile to try to stop your kids from seeing monsters altogether. After all, they are on the front page of the *New York Times* every single day, usually striking a menacing pose. They also frequently commandeer the airwaves during

Saturday-morning cartoons in order to make threatening pronouncements. Short answer: try your best.

What if my child is having nightmares?
Again, this is completely normal. The exception, of course, is when your child has been "marked" by a monster who is using her dreams to try to form a covenant with her. Ask your child for details about her nightmare. Did the monster address her by her Christian name? Was she asked to "sign his book"? If the answer is no, then reassure her it was only a dream, probably.

Should I let my child use a night-light?
A night-light might seem helpful, but experts warn they can do more harm than good. Even a small light can disrupt a child's circadian rhythms and serve as a bull's-eye for the Gauntwings, who cannot hear or smell, and hunt their prey using only their hyperdeveloped sense of sight. The only way to evade the Gauntwings is to live your life in total darkness.

My child is also afraid of the drain. Is *that* normal?

I am going to assume you mean the Drain of Ga, and yes, it's normal for her to be afraid of it. After all, it's a giant, swirling portal in the sky that looks like a screaming mouth. Ever since it first replaced the sun last week, it has been growing in size and anger. Nobody knows where it came from or what's going on with it. It's terrifying.

When my daughter gets upset about monsters, my husband makes jokes to try to cheer her up. I am worried that he is making the problem worse. What do you think?
Your husband is probably a monster. Drug him at dinner, and when he's unconscious, strip his body naked. If he's been "husked," he will have the Mark of Corthar on his chest (see *link*). If he has the mark, cut off his head.

How long will this phase last?
Experts agree that the Age of Monsters is just getting started. There is no end in sight. This is simply the "new normal," and we all have to accept it.

What do I do if I'm feeling overwhelmed?
Don't beat yourself up about it. In these scary haunted times, it's normal to occasionally

feel stressed. If possible, try to carve out some daily "me" time. Maybe it's a glass of wine in the bath while your daughter watches an educational cartoon in the next room? Maybe it's a full bottle of whiskey on the roof while you fire your shotgun at the sky, screaming at the monsters to "just kill me already"? Regardless, it's important to do what you can to manage your anxiety. Otherwise, you might end up "modeling" nervous behavior for your child, which could in turn cause her to experience stress of her own.

Or maybe you should just be straight with her.

What do you mean?

Maybe, when your child asks if something's wrong, you should just tell her the truth: "Yes. Something is very wrong. Monsters are real and they are out there everywhere, trying to kill us."

Won't that freak her out?

She's freaked out already. And she should be. The world as we know it is over, and it's never coming back.

So, what are you saying? What am I supposed to do? Just give up?

You *could* give up.
Or you could fight.

What are you talking about?
I'm talking about taking those monster bastards down.

Whoa, whoa, whoa—hold on. Isn't that impossible?
Maybe. But isn't it worth a shot? Isn't it better than just sitting there, waiting to die?

I can't!
You can.

I'm scared!
I know. But you're stronger than you think. You can do this.

How?
Research the monsters. Learn their weaknesses. Develop a strategy. Stockpile weapons. Train obsessively. Strengthen your body and your mind.

And then what?
When the moment comes, look your child in the

eye. Tell her that the stakes are high, but you're not giving up. Tell her that you will do anything you can to protect her, and even though it's possible you'll fail, you're going to fight for her with everything you've got. Tell her, "If these motherfucking monsters think that they can fuck with my family without me shooting them first in the face, they need to get their heads examined, because I'm going to come at them so fucking hard right now." Watch the strength return to your child as she sees you're in no way fucking around. Listen with pride as she vows to fight the monsters by your side. Look out the window and stare down the monsters together. Dare them to fuck with your family. Dare them to fuck with the people that you love. Take your child by the hand. Arm her to the teeth. Tell her you love her. Open the door.

ACKNOWLEDGMENTS

When writing historical fiction, I always make sure to research the time period extensively and adhere wherever possible to primary sources, except when I want to make a joke or something, in which case I just go ahead and change whatever. The story "Screwball" is a good example of these methods. The premise is true: Jack Dunn really did sign Babe Ruth straight out of St. Mary's, and his nineteen-year-old son, Jack Dunn Jr., really did have the misfortune of competing against Ruth for a roster spot during their joint rookie season. There's no way to know what kind of relationship Dunn Jr. had with Babe Ruth, but when I saw their names printed side by side and looked up their statistics, I couldn't help but try to imagine it. I can't say for sure what percentage of "Screwball" is true, but if I had to put a number on it, I'd guess it's higher than Dunn Jr.'s lifetime batting average, but probably lower than Ruth's. I'm grateful to the following sources for the insight they gave me into Ruth's upbringing and baseball's "dead-ball era."

The Big Bam: The Life and Times of Babe Ruth by Leigh Montville

Babe: The Legend Comes to Life by Robert W. Creamer

Babe Ruth: His Life and Legend by Kal Wagenheim

Humor Among the Minors: True Tales from the Baseball Brush by Edward Michael Ashenback

Fifty-nine in '84 by Edward Achorn

Cobb: A Biography by Al Stump

baseball-reference.com

The rest of the stories are made up.

So many people helped me in so many ways with this book. I want to thank Michael Szczerban, Thea Diklich-Newell, Jayne Yaffe Kemp, Pamela Marshall, Alyssa Persons, Kim Sheu, Daniel Greenberg, Lee Eastman, Gregory McKnight, Allan Haldeman, Alex Rincon, Jonathan Harvey, Robert Webb, Cariad Lloyd, Jamie Demetriou, Lewis Macleod, Freya Parker, Susan Morrison, Emma Allen, David Remnick, Chris Meledandri, Rodney Rothman, Hannah Minghella, Jon Cohen, Jeannette Francis, Daniel Radcliffe, Peter Serafinowicz, Thom Hinkle, Andrew Eisenman, Beck Bennett, Ted Melfi, Mark Johnson, Jim Miller, Erin Westerman, Ryan Reynolds, Phil Lord, Christopher Miller, Paul King, Shana Gohd, Jennifer Kim, Barrett Festen, Gail Winston,

Jake Luce, and the excellent librarians at Shorewood Public Library in Milwaukee, Wisconsin.

Most of all I want to thank my wife, the brilliant writer Kathleen Hale, who has read literally hundreds of versions of these stories. Thank you for making my writing so much better, and the rest of my life, too.

ABOUT THE AUTHOR

Simon Rich is a frequent contributor to *The New Yorker.* He has written for *Saturday Night Live,* Pixar, and *The Simpsons* and is the creator of the TV shows *Man Seeking Woman* and *Miracle Workers,* which he based on his books. His other collections include *Ant Farm, Spoiled Brats,* and *Hits and Misses,* which won the 2019 Thurber Prize for American Humor. He lives in Los Angeles with his family.